CLAWS OF JUSTICE

MINT CHOCOLATE CHIP MYSTERIES

EMMIE LYN

Editor: Helen Page
Proofreader: Alice Shepherd
Cover Designer: Lou Harper, Cover Affairs

Sweet Promise press
PO Box 72
Brighton, MI 48116

To every reader, a heartfelt thank you.
And, a special shout out to Christine M for naming one of
the kitten's in Claws of Justice — Razzleberry.

ABOUT THIS BOOK

I'm Sunny Shaw, and regardless of what my name might suggest, my world has become rather dim as of late.

With a bankrupt business to save, homeless kittens that need rescuing, and a new business partner distracting me with every glance, there seems to be a disaster waiting at every turn.

Just when I thought it couldn't get any worse, a murder literally lands on my doorstep—or at least the corpse does. Now I'm struggling to figure out which problem to solve first!

My business partner seems to want to share more than our lease, but I have to take that step very slowly. Of course, I can't in good conscience leave the kittens to wander the streets. Then again no business means no money.

Decisions. Decisions.

AUTHOR'S NOTE

Hi cozy readers!

Welcome to Pineville in Blueberry Bay on the coast of Maine where cozy mysteries abound. If you've read the Little Dog Diner Cozy Mystery series, you've already met Sunny Shaw and her lovable Newfoundland mix, Jasper. Sunny and Jasper are front and center in the Mint Chocolate Chip Mystery series. Sit back and enjoy. But beware... you're about to fall in love with adorable kittens, be tempted by tasty shakes, and delicious sweets while each story in this exciting series brings you on a twisty turny mystery!

Click here to sign up for my newsletter and never miss a new release.

"Sold!" Police Chief Bullock yelled and pointed in my direction. After watching his performance, I decided that the-middle-aged law enforcement officer loved moonlighting as an auctioneer more than his police responsibilities here in Pineville.

I looked at the people milling around the old Nine Pine Nursery parking lot. Retired couples in baggy jeans and light jackets, millennial owners of local shops, and out-of-towners in designer hiking gear stopping to check for bargains. An event like this, in my quaint Maine town, brought out familiar faces and complete strangers. Some trudged back to their vehicles while others tossed their bidding numbers aside and gathered in groups to chat. I wondered which one of these people just bought this bankrupt business that had once belonged to my grandparents.

"Hey." The gray-haired guy next to me nudged me with his elbow. He hitched his khaki pants over his ample belly and tilted his head toward Chief Bullock. "He means you — Sunny Shaw — right?" He cupped his hand around his mouth as if telling a secret. "I got a peek at the auctioneer's list and put two and two together. Congratulations."

If he hadn't said my name, I would have thought his congratulations was directed to someone else. Anyone else. Instead, I stared, with what I assumed was my mouth dragging on the parking lot and my eyes bugged out.

"What?"

"You just bought this old place. Well, what's left of it, I should say. I did some research and it's a real shame that the previous owner sold off the land. But the retail building is solid, and the glass greenhouse only needs a good cleaning. Nothing some hard work can't fix right up.

Congratulations," he repeated. "I was thinking about buying it myself if I could have gotten it for a song. Didn't happen; you beat my bid. I suppose it's a bit too big for my needs anyway." He looked around wistfully, or so I decided, raised his New York Yankees ball cap and smoothed his thinning hair.

"I did?" This was news to me. I'd only come for entertainment after being canned from my job as the sandwich-wearing lobster who walked up and down Main Street in Pineville, advertising–you won't believe this–a get-away for an all-day cruise around Blueberry Bay. I know it sounds exciting, but believe me, I worked on that cruise and it's full of a rollicking, stomach-upsetting, hang-over-the-railing, seasick six hours. Even my Newfie, Jasper, wasn't a fan. And she loves the water. My ex-boss didn't appreciate that I shared my story with potential fare-paying customers.

"Yeah," the guy said, talking to me like I didn't have a clue. "You need to go up and pay."

Pay? "How much?"

"All of it." He shook his head and must be thinking I was the biggest dimwit he'd ever seen.

"You want some advice?" he asked, dipping his head as if trying to keep his advice from the eaves-dropping public.

At the moment, I wanted answers, not advice but he'd stirred up my endless pit of curiosity. "Sure."

"Watch your back. By the look of this crowd, lots of other people were after this gem." He glanced at his watch, frowned, and walked away without a goodbye.

I bent over to tie my sneaker and think about

what he'd said. Watch my back from what? But, more importantly at the moment, did I have enough money in my bank account to cover this purchase? Definitely not. The inheritance from my great aunt was still tied up in court for the foreseeable future. Maybe a run to the Canadian border was my best option.

Unfortunately, before I even had time to figure out which way was north from the Blueberry Bay area, about a hundred and fifty-five pounds on four legs hit me from behind, squishing me flat into the dirt.

This officially was one of the worst days of my life I said to the rock poking into my cheek.

"Sunny? Open your eyes this minute."

With great effort, I cracked one eyelid a fraction of an inch. "Tilly?" I mumbled. "You brought Jasper here?"

My neighbor, Tilly Morris, stared down at me. Even with all her quirks and wacky ideas, she looked out for me, watched my dog when necessary, and I considered her to be my pistol-packing guardian granny. Of course, I never referred to her that way out loud. She was a tad sensitive about her age—seventy, though you wouldn't know it from her neon wardrobe and oversized personality. And she wasn't anyone's grandmother.

"You sure did get yourself in a pickle this time,

Sunny Shaw," she said as she tugged on my arm.
"Come on. Get up before you catch some disease
from all that dirt you're lying in. What happened to
that guy who was standing next to you? He
disappeared."

I shrugged. Not one bit of all this made a lick of
sense. Something warm and wet traveled from my
chin to my hairline. "Jasper! Stop!" But my dog, a
big Newfoundland mix, the other half something
like a small whale, had launched herself at me when
Tilly brought her into the parking lot. Now she was
straddling me, cleaning every exposed piece of skin
she could find.

"What is so tasty? Did I spill lobster on myself
or something?" I tried to avoid her slobber, but my
best hope of getting away from Jasper's tongue was
to wiggle and squirm out from under her.

With Tilly pulling my arm while Jasper turned
something I'd spilled on myself into her morning
snack, I managed to get on my knees and crawl out
from under her somewhat unusual embrace.

"There," I said, dusting the dirt from my fall in
the parking lot off my khaki capris. I pulled the
elastic out of my ponytail. A quick shake sent bits of
twigs and leaves flying before I twisted my mass of
dark hair into a messy bun, minus the debris. "What
just happened?"

"Apparently, you just bought this property,"

Tilly hissed while pulling me away from all the people. "Are you crazy? How the heck are you planning to pay for it?"

"No worries, Sunny. It's all taken care of."

I almost gave myself whiplash when I turned around at the sound of the one voice that sent shivers up and down my spine. And not in a good way. At least, not anymore. There, smiling at me with green eyes like a cat stalking a mouse, and dimples that always meant trouble, stood Ty Hitchner. At one time I'd hoped he'd be my destiny. But then, he took off for more excitement than he could find with me in Pineville.

Seeing him wasn't good on so many levels.

"Hitch," Tilly said, using his nickname. "Aren't you a sight for sore eyes?" I think she even batted her eyelashes. Ewww.

My neighbor had always thought Hitch was Pineville's gift to women; or, one woman in particular—me. Don't ask me why because Hitch and I had different goals in life. Ever since he'd moved to the Big Apple for what he'd expected to be his dream job as a private security guard, I'd put him out of my mind. *My* goal was to *not* think about Hitch at all. But here he was, looking at me like he'd just returned to save the world. Or, maybe just my world.

I crossed my arms. "What's all taken care of?" I

asked even thought I probably didn't want to know the answer.

"Paying for Nine Pine Nursery." Hitch cocked his head with a quizzical don't-play-dumb look. "You've always said you wished your grandparents hadn't sold it."

"Look, Hitch," I said feeling confused and more than a little frustrated. "I just lost my job, and I have no patience for your games. You were here in Pineville, then you left, and now, here you are again. Don't mess with me."

I blinked back tears that threatened to spill and ruin my tough-girl pose along with a tiny bit of mascara.

Hitch reached out and put his hand on my shoulder. I wished he hadn't done that. How would I possibly resist his charm that he worked like an expert, using that chiseled jaw, those green eyes?

"Sunny," he said with a voice full of compassion. "This is *no* game. I'm back and we just bought the nursery." Then he flashed a grin that normally made my heart flutter. "You can thank me later."

"Wait a minute. We?" Instead of a flutter, my heart pounded, mostly from anger but there might have been a bit of excitement mixed in if I was honest with myself. I patted my chest to calm down this internal battle.

"Yeah, you and me." Hitch spread his hands

across the sky in front of us like he was unraveling a banner. "There's room for both of us. I can see it already—Pineville's new Shakes and Cakes Shop. Sounds great, right? You love those weird smoothies that are all the rave now, and I'll use the greenhouse for my orchid collection and some herbs."

"But—"

He covered my lips with his finger. A finger that smelled like peppermint candy. I closed my eyes, hoping I didn't embarrass myself and take a taste.

"Think about it before you shoot me down," he said, pulling me out of my daydream just in time. "That's all I'm asking, Sunshine. If you don't want to partner with me, I know I can find someone else." He winked, and I knew I was doomed.

A scream pierced the air, which barely entered my consciousness with this latest emotion overload. Tilly raced toward us. I hadn't even registered her absence with Hitch distracting me.

"That guy who was standing next to you?" She looked at me with her big blue eyes wide with fear. Something Tilly rarely showed. "He's dead."

2

—————

"*Who's* dead?" Hitch asked pulling his hand away from my face and treating Jasper to an ear rub instead. Her favorite. She let him know with a loud groan of pleasure that I admit, turned on my jealousy meter.

"The guy who'd been standing next to Sunny during the bidding," Tilly said. She moved her hand in a circular motion. "Come on. Work with me here. He keeled over before he got into his car with a big knife sticking out of his chest. Maxine Salter found him. I swear, you'd think she'd never seen a murder victim before."

"You mean Harry Jenson? The millionaire from New York City? I used to work for him. I saw him standing next to you, Sunny. You know him?" An expression of serious concern transformed his face into his investigative mode, another sideline Hitch enjoyed.

I was still stuck on *murder victim*, never mind the guy's name and address. Who cared about that?

"It's weird. He knew my name, but I never saw the guy before like-fifteen minutes ago. He stood next to me, said a couple of things, then Jasper knocked me over. He told me I outbid him. How did that even happen? *I* never made a bid on anything today."

Boy, was my brain jumping around like a frog in hot water.

Hitch did that cute thing when he knew he was in trouble, tucking his chin down and rolling his eyes. "I kind of used your name when I got my bidding number, Sunny. I told Police Chief Bullock I wanted to surprise you, but I put up the money. Some surprise, right?"

Hitch looked at me like I should bow with thanks in front of him. It was hard to still be furious, but a *thanks* was not happening.

"Yeah, some surprise," I said but apparently without the requisite level of enthusiasm based on Ty's crestfallen face. He couldn't have everything. Right now, his revelation made my head spin. How could I be part owner of what used to be the Nine Pine Nursery? And if that wasn't enough, I was trying to process Tilly's shocking news.

"He was *murdered*?" Practically right under my nose. The reality of the situation hit me harder than a tidal wave.

"Hitch?" Tilly said, pulling us away from the crowd of gawkers. "Maybe we can sneak away before Officer Walker arrives and starts asking questions. You and I both know what that will mean."

"That's the best thing I've heard all day," Hitch said and picked up the pace. With Hitch on one side and Tilly on the other, I couldn't resist being swept along.

We almost made it.

Officer Mick Walker's SUV screeched to a stop, cutting us off from what Tilly liked to call her getaway vehicle—a lime green Volkswagen bug that matched her jogging outfit. Not that Tilly did much jogging, but she liked to be color coordinated. Shocking, right? Her theory—be as noticeable as possible. But I never understood her logic.

Mick pointed at us through the dirty windshield of his Pineville police department vehicle and shook his head. He wasn't my favorite person in Pineville, but for Hitch? They'd always butted heads, mostly over me.

Mick exited his SUV and walked over to our little threesome while finger combing his crew cut of sun-bleached hair.

Ty whispered to me, "Don't admit to anything, he'll be fishing for information."

I shielded my eyes from the bright sun as I waited to hear what Mick had up his sleeve.

"Interesting goings-on around here this morning," Mick said. The toothpick he always kept at the corner of his mouth bobbed up and down while he spoke.

For some reason, that toothpick looked like it had a life of its own. I tried to choke back a laugh. Of course, it didn't work and what sounded more like a honking goose slipped out.

"Something's funny?" Mick's toothpick motion paused as his jaw clenched.

Tilly, always looking out for me, tapped her chin then pointed to Mick. "Did you have eggs for breakfast?"

Wow. I'd totally missed that but once again, she'd saved me from my lack of self-restraint. With the back of his hand, Mick rubbed away a big yellow yolk smear. Without even showing a bit of embarrassment, he continued. "Police Chief Bullock called every available officer here to help with the current situation."

"What situation?" I asked. I'd made the quick decision to pretend I knew nothing about any guy or any murder. "We're on our way to Tilly's house to discuss a new business venture."

Hitch grabbed my hand and squeezed it tight, forcing me to look at him. He clamped his lips together and gave me a quick head shake. I guess our business venture was supposed to stay secret.

Mick's eyebrows shot out of sight under his mop. He crossed his arms and leaned his long, angular frame against his SUV. "I can't wait to hear those details. I mean, I heard you were just canned from your job, and you already have a business venture in place? Does it have anything to do with… oh… I don't know… Nine Pine Nursery?"

"Really, Mick," Tilly said, "it's not any of your business, so how about you let us get on with ours."

"That's where you're wrong, Tilly. A rich guy from New York had his eye on the nursery. Now, he's dead. And, what a coincidence that Mr. Hitchner is back in town putting up the money to buy the nursery that, just so happens, used to be in Sunny's family." He paused, taking a good long look at each of us. "Putting all that together, does make your business my business. Let's go, Sunny."

"But—"

His glare shut me up.

"Jasper's coming with me," I said. That was not negotiable.

Mick led me inside the building attached to the greenhouse. My building now, I thought with some satisfaction even though I was inside for all the wrong reasons. I could totally imagine transforming it into a snazzy spot to serve crazy shakes and little sweet cakes.

Mick pointed to a chair and said, "Sit."

A pathetic mew caught my attention. Under my chair was the cutest, most adorable, but terrified kitty I'd ever seen. Well, to be honest, all kittens are adorable. Ignoring Mick, I reached down and scooped the soft fur ball into my arms. "Where'd you come from?"

Jasper nosed the kitten who batted back at the monster. The kitty settled in my arms and purred as I massaged behind her ears. My brain took a giant leap. This place could also house stray kittens. I wondered what Princess Muffin, my gray tabby kitty, would think of that idea before I even considered what Hitch would have to say. If we were going to be partners, that meant I had as much to say about what we did with this place as he did. I smiled at this vision of shakes, cakes, and kitties.

"Sunny!" Mick leaned right in my face and lowered his voice. "Wipe that grin off your face. You're in a heap of trouble. What were you and the victim talking about just before he was killed?"

I looked into the kitty's blue eyes hoping she had some answers for me.

"Sunny?" Mick touched my arm.

I jumped. What the heck was happening?

3

The noise suddenly ratcheted up several decibels in this place. Whoops. This post and beam building of rough-cut pine belonged to Hitch and me now, I reminded myself. Our building was getting crowded. Three state policemen entered the space and headed straight toward Police Chief Bullock.

Mick stood at attention when he spotted them. He gave me a serious look I couldn't decipher and said, "I'll be back."

"This is our investigation now," one of the state policemen said. That would be the tallest, leanest, and meanest-sounding of the three.

I walked around the perimeter of the room unnoticed by the law enforcement conference going on. I didn't see any signs the kitty had a home in the corner, a snug nest with her mother or bowls of water or food anywhere. My guess is she was a stray.

Lucky for me that all attention was on this new power trip unfolding just a few feet away. If the Pineville Police weren't in charge, this was my cue to sneak out. After a quick look at the policemen arguing and finger-pointing behind *my* oak counter, which needed a sanding, I noticed, and a coat of polyurethane to bring it back to life, I made my move.

Without further ado, and mustering all the confidence I possessed, I tucked my new kitty into my sweatshirt pocket, snapped my fingers at Jasper, and skirted around the edge of the room and out the door.

I expected to hear Mick's booming voice ordering me to stop, but apparently, my luck had changed. No one even batted an eye in my direction.

My new kitty didn't complain about her unconventional hiding spot, which gave me an idea. "How about the name Stash?" I asked Jasper as soon as we were out in the sunshine and fresh air.

"Who are you talking to?" Hitch stepped out from the shadow of the overhang on our new building, scaring me right out of my sneakers. Almost. "Come on," he said. Not waiting for a response, he looped his arm through mine and more or less dragged me straight toward Tilly's VW bug.

Hitch opened the passenger door for me. "I'll follow you two to Tilly's house."

I pointed to Jasper and pulled Stash out of my pocket. "Four." I corrected him.

"Four what?"

"Four of us — Tilly and me, plus Jasper and Stash."

His face softened as he looked at Stash with an, "Aww," and fluffed her soft fur. "How on earth did you add to your menagerie while you were with Mick?" Hitch shook his head. "Never mind. We'll talk at Tilly's house."

Cats just happened to be one of Hitch's soft spots. He'd never be able to say no to my cat shelter idea.

"I'm not sure I like what's going on in your head right now, Sunny. You have that look that tells me you've got a plan which usually leads to trouble."

"You'll love it," I answered and tipped the seat forward for Jasper to squeeze into the back. "Trust me," I added with a big grin.

"Love what?" Tilly asked when I'd settled on the passenger seat with my newest family member.

"Meet Stash!" I held up my blue-eyed, velvet-soft, gray and white kitty. "She's going to help us solve the murder of," I looked at Tilly, "what was his name?" I didn't really believe she'd help, but the idea was appealing.

"Harry Jenson." Tilly, a strong, take-no-prisoners kind of woman, spit the name out like it was toxic. I realized she knew something about the guy, which didn't sit well with her. In a big way.

"Who is Harry Jenson?" I asked, cuddling Stash under my chin and enjoying the ticklish purring vibration. "Don't think I didn't notice the glance you and Hitch shared."

"It's complicated," Tilly said, staring straight ahead. "For now, I suppose all you need to know is that Hitch worked for him in New York until their relationship took a turn for the worst and that's why Hitch is back here in Pineville. Well, that and he missed you." She peeked at me, the key in her hand, her foot on the brake, but I pretended not to notice.

Hitch was back because he missed me? He'd have to earn back my friendship. And buying Nine Pine Nursery for me wouldn't do it. Money couldn't buy my love. It was a step in the right direction, though.

"You're grinning, Sunny."

"Wouldn't you grin too if you had this soft fur ball nestled under your chin?" Great avoidance, I told myself proudly. "See what I mean." I held Stash on Tilly's shoulder so she could hear Stash's motor and feel the kitten's whiskers tickle her neck.

Tilly smiled and leaned into Stash's softness. "Okay, you made your point," she said as she put the key in the ignition and started the VW. "But try not to push Hitch out of your life just because he moved away to follow his dream in NYC."

Getting her beloved bug out into traffic without a hitch, pardon the pun, took her attention for a moment. Once she had her baby purring in fourth gear away from the nursery, she said, "He's gonna need help from both of us now. Don't think for a second that Officer Mick Walker isn't going to try to pin this murder on him. Even though the state police arrived to take over the investigation, Mick will figure out a way to weasel into the investigation. He always does."

"I thought Mick was looking for a different job. Out of law enforcement?"

"My sources told me, with Hitch back in town, Mick's not going anywhere."

Great. Just when I thought Mick would be out of my life, I had to keep avoiding his overbearing toxic presence. Mick Walker was a bully and knew exactly how to play the system to get what he wanted. He'd made it plain that he wanted me but that would never happen.

Hitch arrived home and landed in a mess.

4

---

*H*itch's metallic blue Camaro, his pride and joy, was already parked outside of Tilly's small ranch house when we arrived on Cobbler Lane.

"How'd he beat us here?" I asked. "Wasn't he behind us the whole way?"

Tilly chuckled. "You were too busy cooing to that new ball of fur you found. I saw him cut through the abandoned road and leave a cloud of dust behind. I hope he didn't rip off his exhaust system on that unused bumpy cow path."

I reached for Tilly's arm, preventing her from sliding out before I could ask her a question. "Tell me, Tilly, why is Hitch really back in town?"

She dropped her head, not looking at me. "It's complicated. There's a lot Hitch made me promise not to tell you." Finally, with great effort, she met my gaze. "What I *can* say is that coming back to Pineville is where he needs to be right now. If this new business venture pans out, he'll be here to stay."

"That's a big *if*, isn't it?" I said with a sinking feeling in the pit of my stomach.

Tilly placed her rough, sun-spotted hand over mine. "I won't lie and tell you that you two will live happily ever after, but if something is important, you have to fight for it." She squeezed my hand. "Come on, step one is to be patient until Hitch is ready to tell you what happened in New York."

The only thing left to do, was open the door and face whatever waited. Jasper happily jumped out of Tilly's cramped back seat and headed across the street to my house.

"Jasper. This way," I called to her with no luck. "Here." I handed Stash to Tilly. "Something's up with Jasper. Get some coffee going, and I'll be right over."

"Don't expect scones with that coffee, Sunny. Or anything else for that matter. You know that I can barely cook to save my life, and baking? Not in my skill set."

"You don't need to remind me. I ended up in the ER with salmonella poisoning after I ate one of your brownies from a mix. I still haven't figured out how *that* could even happen. I'll bring something over from my house." I jogged to catch up to Jasper who was already headed around the side of my house to the back door where I'd installed a giant doggy door for her. She was no dummy.

Jasper disappeared inside.

I fished around in my pocket for my key. Nothing. I even pulled it inside out. Still nothing. Why, at this moment, when everything was already topsy-turvy, did I lose my key?

I looked at Jasper's doggy door. At least it was the extra-large size. I sighed, dropped onto my hands and knees and pushed the flap open. "Jasper? Everything okay in there?" I called with my head inside and my rear end still outside.

A big slobbery tongue swiped my face.

Laughter erupted behind me.

Seriously? Someone caught me in this compromising position? I scooched backwards to see who I was up against.

"Is this what you need?" Hitch dangled a key from one finger after I stood up. "Found it at Tilly's house."

"Actually, it's part of my daily exercise routine, keeps me flexible." I certainly wasn't giving him the satisfaction of commenting on whether my rear fit through the doggy door or not. It would if it had to.

"If you say so, Sunny." Hitch didn't even try to

hide his smirk as he unlocked my door and held his hand out for me to go inside first. "Tilly asked me to check that everything was okay over here. Does she know about your... exercise routine? I'd say that this gives a new twist to the downward dog yoga position."

I ignored him and put my shoulder bag on the counter before I said something stupid and shoved my foot farther down my throat. Instead, I changed the subject and put Hitch on the spot. "What happened in New York?"

Hitch leaned against my kitchen sink and stared out the window into my backyard. "It's complicated."

"Yeah, that's what Tilly told me. Since you don't want to be honest with me, I'll make up my own story of what happened. How does this sound?"

I heard the snippiness in my voice, but Hitch had no right to come waltzing back into my life like everything was smelling like roses. In fact, every-thing was inside out and upside down. "That guy, Harry, came to Pineville looking for you and now he's dead. Mick will put you at the top of the suspect list and do whatever he can to put you in jail because Officer Mick Walker wants you out of my life. Well?"

Hitch turned around and stared at the floor. "That's not exactly what's going on except for the part about Mick wanting me out of your life. I think you hit that nail on the head," he said sounding defeated.

Okay. Hitch was hurting. Tilly said he needed our help. I couldn't turn my back on him, especially when he sounded so vulnerable. I was a sap for a guy showing me his emotions.

I moved next to him and took his hand in both of mine. "Level with me... please."

Hitch inhaled deeply and exhaled slowly. "I worked for Harry in New York. During a shootout, I got hit and left my job with a big insurance payoff."

"Shot?" my heart almost stopped. "No one told me."

"That's the way I wanted it. When I decided to come back here, I didn't want your pity. I want your friendship, Sunny." He raised his head. His green eyes pleaded with me.

"Right. I'm not the pitying type, you big dork." I grinned and punched Hitch's arm. He flinched.

"It's not healed yet. If you have to punch me again, hit my other arm, okay?"

"You got shot in your arm?"

"Just one."

And there I saw it—Hitch's grin that melted my heart. The tension between us, gone, our old, easy-going relationship, back.

"But, I'm still confused why Harry came to Pineville. He told me he was interested in buying Nine Pine Nursery. Was that for real?"

"Let's sit down, Sunny. This story has several parts."

I led him into my living room where Jasper was sprawled on the floor with Princess Muffin attacking her big fluffy tail.

"Sunny? You have kittens everywhere I turn? Are there more?"

"Well, I do have an idea for our business venture, but first I want to hear the rest of the details about you." I leveled my best serious glare at him. "No changing the subject."

Hitch scooped up Princess Muffin and settled his lanky frame on my couch and tucked her in the crook of his arm. "What's her name?" he asked.

"Hitch? Nice try but get back to the shooting details, and then I'll tell you her name."

"Harry shot me."

That was the last thing I expected to hear and probably the worst answer considering the situation we'd just left behind us.

How long before that incident caught up with Hitch?

"*H*arry *shot* you?" was all I managed to say.

My kitchen door slammed, and I heard footsteps approaching. "What happened to the two of you?" Tilly shouted. "Did you forget about me and my coffee?"

"Does she know?" I whispered to Hitch.

He nodded.

"Oh," Tilly said after she took one look at what had to be our glum expressions. She set the coffee carafe on my little side table. "Here, I brought some magic to cheer you up." She pulled Stash out of her pocket. "This little puffball has been sleeping in here since you handed her to me."

"Poor thing." I took her in my arms and stroked her soft fur. She rewarded me with a satisfied purr, a magic spell that instantly made me feel better. "She must have been terrified in that big empty abandoned building."

Stash stood on all fours, arched her back, and jumped off my lap, curling up between Jasper's big front paws. Jasper sniffed the tiny kitten and wagged her tail, which made Princess Muffin jump out of Hitch's arm and pounce again.

"Well, look at that—Jasper, the kitten whisperer. Stash and Jasper are best friends already. Jasper can be the nanny in our new Kitty Castle." From Hitch's raised eyebrows, I remembered that I hadn't shared my plan with him yet. "There's plenty of room for your orchids and my shakes and cakes *plus* kitties."

"I'll get the mugs while you two sort this out." Tilly snorted on her way to the kitchen. For once, she didn't add her two cents worth to the conversation.

Hitch leaned back and stretched both arms along the back of the couch. He cocked his head. "Please. Fill me in on this Kitty Castle idea of yours, Sunny. I can't wait to hear the details."

I pointed at him. "Not yet, Hitch. First, the rest about you getting shot." My voice sounded shrill even to my own ears.

Tilly returned with three mugs, setting them down next to the coffee with a thud. "It's about time you finally told her. Now, help yourselves. I'm Sunny's neighbor not her maid."

I loved the no-nonsense way Tilly had about her. Hitch, on the other hand, looked like he felt a little outnumbered. The coffee aroma overwhelmed my already buzzing nerves, so I passed on coffee and only filled two mugs.

Tilly helped herself to one, asking, "Any idea why Harry came to Pineville?"

"I've got a theory," Hitch said, ignoring the other mug of coffee. "When I was working for him, I mentioned Pineville. To my surprise, he said he had a friend who lived here. If he ever left New York, he said he'd look at moving to Pineville. After the shooting, he said he was done with the city. He was ready to find someplace quiet, off the beaten trail, where he could enjoy his plant obsession without the worry of another break-in."

"Who's the friend?" Tilly asked, sliding to the edge of her wooden rocker.

"At the time, I didn't ask him who it was." Hitch scooped up Princess Muffin and gave me an eyebrow wiggle. "Your turn, Sunny. What's the name of this piece of fluff?"

He still hadn't told me much about the shooting, but I'd get it out of him sooner or later. I could play this game, too. "That is the stunning Princess Muffin. Tilly's friend, Nan, who lives in Glendale brought over a litter of kittens. I had the toughest time picking only one, but Jasper helped. She bonded immediately with this cutie-patootie. Now, no more distractions, Hitch. Back to your story. Why did Harry shoot you?"

Hitch rubbed his arm as his eyes glazed over, obviously going back in time. Princess Muffin provided a calming backdrop of purrs while Hitch transported himself back to the shooting scene in New York City.

"Harry said it was an accident, which tells me that anyone *that* careless shouldn't be allowed anywhere near a gun." He picked up the mug of coffee and sipped, still lost in his memory.

He finally continued. "I was on duty the night of the break-in when we heard a noise in Harry's special plant room just before midnight. I rushed in first since the whole reason I was there was to protect his orchid collection and some centuries old valuable bonsai plant. He claimed it was worth more than I'd ever earn in a lifetime. I had everything under control—the intruder in my crosshairs—but Harry," Hitch spit out the name angrily, "fired from behind me, hitting my arm. The bone got nicked and the muscle is still weak and sore. The intruder escaped."

I looked at his arm, covered by a long-sleeve t-shirt and had the horrid thought that maybe today,

Harry got exactly what he deserved—a type of justice. But who delivered that death penalty?

"I know what you're thinking, Sunny," Hitch said, interrupting my thoughts. "He got what he deserved. Part of me agrees with that, but now I'll never get closure about why he pulled the trigger when he did." He drained his mug and lifted one shoulder. "It is what it is. Now, I have to be sure Officer Walker doesn't figure out how to tie me to Harry's death."

"What could he have on you, Hitch?" Tilly asked as if this was one ridiculous worry. "Sure, you were at the auction, but so were about fifty other people, including Sunny and me. Mick would have to find someone who saw you near Harry."

I was thinking in a different direction. "Who was that intruder? Maybe he or she followed Harry here to Pineville to finish unfinished business."

"The intruder wore a mask. All I know is the person was shorter than me, maybe five feet seven or eight, wore white sneakers and black clothes. Not much to go on. That person had planned a theft, not murder. And, the white sneakers make me think the person wasn't a seasoned burglar."

I stood up and stretched all the kinks out. "That leaves the people at the auction. Where were you standing?" I asked Hitch. "Did you see Harry with anyone?"

He wouldn't look at me.

"You did see him, didn't you?"

Hitch nodded and grimaced. "Yeah, I saw him standing next to you. When he was alone, I let him know exactly what I thought of him and told him to get out of town."

Oh boy, that wasn't what I wanted to hear. Who else overheard that argument? I wondered.

6

*S*omeone pounded on my front door, and all three of us turned as one. Jasper barked loud enough to rattle the windows. The kitties charged for safety under the couch.

"Who is it?" I asked Tilly who had the best view to the street.

"It looks like a couple of the state policemen that we saw after Harry was killed. Hitch, go in the kitchen. This is Sunny's house, so they aren't looking for you. I'll stay here with Sunny." She grinned at us. "I'm just a little old lady with no memory and not much common sense."

I opened the door a crack. "Yes?"

"Ms. Shaw? I'm Detective Marsh and this is Detective Cooper." They both flipped open their badges for me to see. "Can we come in?"

"As long as you don't mind my dog." It was all I could do to hold Jasper from pushing her big head between me and the door opening.

When I pulled the door open far enough for them to come inside, the policemen's eyes popped open wider than their shiny badges. "A dog?" Detective Marsh squeaked.

Jasper barked, letting them know that's exactly what she was plus she'd added a little extra warning in her woof.

Detective Cooper walked right in and let Jasper sniff his hand. Great. Now they'd know she was all bark and no bite.

"Sunny, honey. I need help in the bathroom," Tilly said. When I turned to look at her she had her knees together as she shifted her weight from one foot to the other. "Right now."

"Uh..." I looked at the detectives. "Sorry. I'll be right back."

With Tilly leaning on me, we hobbled down the hall to the bathroom. I slammed the door closed. "What the heck are you doing?"

"Letting them know you have your hands full. They'll be in and out of your hair in two shakes of a wet towel."

I flushed the toilet in case they were listening and helped Tilly back to the rocking chair by the front window. She muttered to herself the whole time. It was all I could do to keep from kicking her in the shins to be quiet. I wasn't sure she was helping at all.

The two detectives stood right inside the door with Jasper sitting watch in front of them.

"We'll only take a minute of your time, Ms. Shaw," Detective Cooper said. "Did you know Harry Jenson?"

"No," I answered.

"But you were seen standing with him and talking to him before the final bid at the Nine Pine Nursery auction. How do you explain that?" He cocked his head and looked down at me.

"Easy. He spoke to me, and I answered. That's what polite people do in Pineville. Then he walked away." I stared right at Detective Cooper letting him know he didn't intimidate me in the least. It would have been intimidating if I actually had something to hide, but I didn't.

"What exactly did he say to you?"

I put my finger over my lips like I had to think long and hard about that. "Well, not much really. He said he was hoping to buy Nine Pine Nursery, but I beat his bid."

Princess Muffin, curious now that the barking had stopped, jumped on Jasper's tail, distracting me from the seriousness of the situation.

Tilly said, "Do I know you two handsome men?

Would you like to come back for dinner? You could bring me some nice Chinese take-out."

"I'm sorry, Ma'am. What's your name?" Detective Cooper asked.

"Tilly. It's my nickname. I never liked my real name much." She continued to rock like a maniac.

"And were you at the auction this morning?"

"The auction. Was I, Sunny?"

"Yes, Tilly. You came with Jasper, remember?"

Tilly's eyes lit up. "That's right. That nice man Harry told me I have pretty eyes." Tilly fluttered her eyelashes at the detectives. "Don't I, Detective?"

I almost threw up.

Detective Marsh jabbed Detective Cooper in the side. "Thanks for your time, ladies." Then Detective Marsh handed me his card. "If you remember anything else, please give me a call. Anything at all, you never know what could be important."

They turned to leave but apparently Tilly hadn't finished having fun with them.

"Wait. I just remembered something. That man you just asked about? I think I might have seen him talking to Maxine Salter."

"Did you or didn't you?" Detective Marsh asked with more than a touch of irritation in his voice.

"Yes, I did. I'm sure of it." Tilly tapped her head. "This old memory isn't what it used to be, but I know

Maxine and she had on her I-mean-business outfit of hot pink with her purple hat. When she wears that, you can be sure that she's out and about ready to accomplish something. She had that poor man almost backed into the woods at the edge of the parking lot. I don't know if they were talking or arguing but there was a lot of finger pointing going on. Does that help?" She even fluttered her eyelashes again.

"It might. Thank you again. We'll let ourselves out." Detective Marsh opened the door and was out before Tilly had a chance to come up with any more of her observations.

The police car hadn't even driven off when Hitch came out of the kitchen. "Did you just make that up, Tilly?"

"Of course not. Maxine definitely had on her hot pink outfit and that hideous purple hat she always wears for important occasions." She leaned close to the window and waved.

I couldn't believe it!

"What about the other part? You didn't tell us that before," Hitch said. "Was she really arguing with Harry?"

"I didn't tell you because you never asked me what I saw. Not like those two handsome detectives did. Yes. Maxine was talking to Harry at the edge of the parking lot. I might have exaggerated a bit about the finger waving part, but I don't think they'll arrest me for that."

Hitch shook his head. I wasn't sure if he was about to laugh or walk out. He didn't do either. Instead, he sat down and finished his coffee.

"What on earth does Maxine have to do with this Harry guy?" I was beginning to feel like this whole tangled mess was connected somehow but I couldn't see any logical explanation.

"Maxine is the president of the orchid society here in Pineville," Hitch said. "With Harry's orchid collection, it makes perfect sense that he would talk to her."

"Don't forget, Maxine was the first one to find his body," Tilly said, so excited she was bouncing on the balls of her feet.

"You think she killed him?"

"I don't know but I'll put money down that she knows something," Tilly said, ready to charge forward after information.

I agreed, but *what* did Maxine know?

7

"Slow down a minute, you two," Hitch said, pulling the emergency brake on our rush to the front door. "We need a plan. If we all go charging over to Maxine's house, she'll be suspicious. I think I should go since I have orchid collecting in common with her."

"And, you worked for Harry, so you have that in common, too," I said. "Although, you might not want to play that card yet."

"Whatever," Tilly said with a flap of her hand. "I'm taking my coffee carafe back to my house while you two do your little dance around the suspect pole."

I looked at Hitch and raised my eyebrows. "What's that supposed to mean?" I whispered.

He shrugged.

Tilly opened the door. "Well, look at who just showed up at my house for a visit."

"Maxine?" both Hitch and I blurted out.

"No. She'd rather die than set foot in the same room with me. My friend from Misty Harbor, Sue Ellen Baer is walking to my front door. And, it looks like she has a handsome man with her. Toodle-oo you two. I've got to meet that hunk on her arm."

I grabbed Hitch's arm, the good one, and pulled him outside. "We have to stay with Tilly before she does something impulsive like barge in on Maxine and accuse her of murder."

Jasper trotted along with us, but the kittens watched from the windowsill.

Tilly jogged across the street and hollered, "Sue Ellen!" She waved her arms to get her friend's attention, in case the screech wasn't enough.

Sue Ellen, dressed in a red flowery dress, turned and a big grin spread across her face. She waved. "I was afraid I wouldn't find you here. Is this a bad time for a visit, Tilly?"

"Not at all." "Who's your handsome friend?"

The man smiled and stuck his hand out. "Conrad Coleman. Pleased to meet you. Sue Ellen has told me so much about her beautiful friend." Conrad kissed Tilly's outstretched hand.

"Oh, please," she giggled. Even from half-way across the street, I saw pink travel straight up her neck to the tips of her ears.

When Hitch and I caught up, I offered my hand in a no-nonsense manner. "Sunny Shaw, Tilly's neighbor, and this is my friend, Ty Hitchner."

Conrad shook my hand. No kiss, thank goodness. Then, after a slight pause, he shook Hitch's hand.

Sue Ellen leaned close to Tilly and whispered like they were a couple of teenagers discussing some sort of naughty deed. "I heard there's been some excitement in your town. If I know you, Tilly Morris, you'll have more details than anyone else."

"Well, maybe a few more." Tilly looked up and down the street.

Was she checking that the coast was clear?

She wrapped her arm around Sue Ellen's shoulders. "Let's go inside. We've already had a visit from the state police and there's no sense in rousing their suspicion from a gathering out here."

"Oh, you make this sound so cloak and dagger-like. Are you involved?" Sue Ellen giggled as Tilly led her inside.

"After you," Hitch said and took up the rear behind Conrad and me.

"So," Tilly said, unloading her carafe on me to

deal with. "What brings you to Pineville, Sue Ellen? I hope it's not just the murder."

Sue Ellen sat in Tilly's comfy recliner and popped the footrest up. "Don't be silly. Didn't you get my message?"

I glanced at Tilly's answering machine. The telltale red light flashed so I hit the play button. Sue Ellen's voice rang out. *"Coming with my friend, Conrad, who has some business to take care of in Pineville. Hope to see you, too, my dear."*

Sue Ellen held her hands out. "And, here we are. Conrad's the contractor I told you about. You said you wanted to do a bathroom remodel. He'd love to take a look and give you a quote.

While Tilly and Sue Ellen chatted, Hitch pulled me aside. "Listen, Sunny. This is a good time for us to get out of here and visit Maxine. What do you think?"

"You want me to come with you?"

"I think it's less intimidating if we go together as a couple of friends looking for some orchid info. I mean, we've got the old nursery now, so we can use that as a starting point."

"Okay. I like it. How about Jasper? Bring her or leave her here with Tilly?"

"Leave her here."

I nodded. "Hey, Tilly? Since your friends are

here, Hitch and I are going to do some business planning. We can catch up with you later."

A flash of something—annoyance?—passed over her face. She hated being left out, but she couldn't very well abandon her friend who'd just shown up out of the blue.

"Before you go," Tilly said, "Sue Ellen says Conrad is one of the best contractors around. Keep him in mind when you make your plans for your remodeling."

Conrad smiled broadly and handed me his business card. "Yes, please give me a call. From the little bit I've already heard, I'd be honored to have the chance to help you transform that old nursery into a shiny new business."

I slipped his card into my pocket. "Of course. We'd love to hear your thoughts once we have more details hammered out. Right, Hitch?"

"Sure," he said with little enthusiasm. Whatever. It was a business decision we both had to make together.

On our drive, I asked Hitch, "When do you want to get started with some real planning for our new business venture?" I mean, ideas were flying around in my head like a hungry school of sharks— crazy shake combos, sweet and pretty cakes, and of course, the Kitty Castle.

"I thought you'd never ask. How about after we

talk to Maxine? Then, you can tell me all your ideas. I only have one requirement."

"Which is?"

"That's easy. I get to sample all your creations."

He looked at me with his irresistible grin and I knew I was in big trouble.

8

*H*itch turned into a driveway that led to a rambling modernized farmhouse — red metal roof, wraparound porch, and a cobblestone path to the front door. Blueberry Bay glistened through the trees in the distance. The manicured lawn surrounded a shallow pool with a leaping dolphin statue in the center. It all reeked of more money than I'd ever see in several lifetimes. Even after my great-aunt's inheritance arrived.

"We're just going to knock on her door?" I asked Hitch. "This place looks like it's guarded by someone ready to send us packing, don't you think?"

He laughed but stroked my cheek reassuringly. "She won't bite. I know Maxine. She's exactly like Harry. More money than they know what to do with, but they're still human with flaws and desires like the rest of us."

"Flaws?" I leaned away from Hitch, aghast. "What are *mine*?"

"Yours are more like cute blemishes that just make your whole package more appealing." He tapped my chin affectionately.

His smile made my heart thump at double speed. I pushed the car door open to escape this conversation before I spontaneously burst into flames.

"Just let me do the talking." Hitch looked at me over the roof of his Camaro. "I'll pour on my love of orchids and invite her to host the next orchid society meeting."

"What do you know about the orchid society?" He raised an eyebrow, so I knew he was concocting a story on the spot. "You're making this up as you go along, aren't you?"

He hitched the collar of his polo shirt, a move that always made me a little weak in the knees. "Let me finish," he said in his teasing way. "As I was saying, I'll invite her to host a meeting of the society, which I'm about to join, at our new and remodeled Orchid Extravaganza."

I'd started up the walk to the heavy front door of Maxine's house but that stopped me in my tracks. "Orchid Extravaganza? That's the name you've chosen?" I nodded, liking the sound of it. "That works."

"For now," Hitch said sounding more confident in this scheme than I was. "Anyway, our goal today is to get inside to see her collection. Trust me. She'll invite us in."

I had my doubts, but we'd see how well Hitch's charm worked.

As we followed the cobblestone path to the front door, the lush mix of pink and white roses climbing up the porch balustrades released a heady aroma that had me swooning. The layers of heirloom blossoms belonged on a design magazine cover and had me salivating with envy.

Hitch nudged me and pointed to the entryway. "There's her guard dog you were so worried about." A big stone dog sat to one side of the front door with a basket of purple petunias flowing over the sides. "I guess you don't have to worry about Maxine threatening us after all."

"Yeah, well, that's only the first warning. What's on the inside?" I asked but Hitch only laughed.

He pushed the doorbell and deep chimes rang somewhere behind the door.

I pulled on his arm. "She's not home. Let's go." I pulled harder but his muscular body didn't even budge an inch.

"What are you so nervous about, Sunny?" he

asked. Easy for him to say. He towered over me and with his security guard training, could handle any emergency coming at us once that door opened.

I peeked through the narrow pane of glass next to the door then scurried back. "She's coming. What if she killed Harry? What if *she's* the murderer? Are we walking right into a trap?"

Ty's face gave nothing away. I tried to adopt his calm attitude. "We're here to talk about orchids," he said. "Relax. Maxine will be on her best behavior regardless of what she did or didn't do. She does *not* want to look guilty of anything. Trust me."

"Famous last words," I mumbled.

The door opened. Maxine appeared in a flourish of arm-waving and eye-brow-raising coquettish welcoming movements. "Ty Hitchner? How wonderful to see you back in town. Tell me, are you still collecting orchids?" Her crown of bleached blonde straw hovered shoulder-length, too stiff to do much more than stand at attention from too much hair spray. She held her arm out, inviting us inside with a slight bow in my direction. "Sunny Shaw? How's your friend, Tilly Morris?" Her smile was like a winter sun, light in those blue eyes but no warmth.

She just asked about the person she wouldn't set foot in the same room with? I had no idea how I was supposed to answer that, except short and sweet.

"She's fine." I added a smile, too. It couldn't hurt to let her know I was friendly and not here for some sinister purpose. I hoped she couldn't see through my nervous shuffling from foot to foot.

The door clicked closed behind us and sent a jarring shot of fear up my spine. Hitch took my hand. His quiet strength helped calm my frayed nerves. I looked at Maxine with her oddly coiffed bob, hot pink linen skirt, and cream-colored silk blouse fitting snugly on her sleek figure. Definitely not the ensemble of a killer. I'd follow Hitch's lead on this.

Hitch started the conversation going. "My obsession with orchids has only increased, Maxine. You know, now that I've moved back to Pineville, I'd love to join your orchid society." I could tell she was dazzled by Hitch's smile. She didn't take her blue eyes tinged with suspicion off him.

He said, "Is there any chance you'd give us a teeny peek of your collection?" He had the merest suggestion of flirtation in his voice.

Conflicting emotions battled on her face.

He jumped in to ease the moment. "Of course, since we dropped in unexpectedly, I completely understand if you don't have time." He leaned close to her and said, in a conspiratorial fashion, "But, couldn't you spare a few minutes? And, I'd be happy to show you mine sometime."

That last comment came out wrong in my opinion, but it made Maxine chuckle and seemed to warm her up to Hitch.

She gave him a friendly nudge in the ribs. "You haven't lost that famous charm, have you, Ty Hitchner. Follow me. I have a few minutes to spare."

She led us through a maze of doorways into a sun-filled room, chatting away about orchids the whole time. A glass dome overhead, and floor to ceiling windows, made for the perfect backdrop for the most amazingly beautiful plants I'd ever seen. The sound of gurgling water added to the tropical garden atmosphere. I was enchanted.

"Stunning," Hitch said and from his rapt expression I knew he meant it.

I couldn't move from the tiled step as I took in the beauty that surrounded me. Butterflies even fluttered between feeding stations and flowers. One delicately floated down and landed on my shoulder.

I looked at Hitch with my eyes wide with the excitement of a toddler. "I don't believe this."

Maxine chuckled. "Sunny, that Blue Morph butterfly found a friend. Some people believe it symbolizes good luck. I'm not sure I believe that based on my day today. But," she waved her hand dismissively, "never mind about that. Come down here, and I'll show you something else that's pretty special." Her high-heeled sandals click-clacked on the colorful tiles on her path across the room.

I glanced at Hitch and whispered. "What did she mean by that?"

Without answering, he said, "Maxine, I think we might have a mutual orchid lover in common. Do you know Harry Jensen?"

I held back on the step, wondering where this was headed.

Maxine spun around, but her hair didn't move an inch. "I think you mean, *had*, Ty. We *had* a mutual orchid lover in common. He was murdered this morning." Her mouth tightened at the corners. "As I think you both already know since you were at the auction, too."

No kidding, I almost blurted out. Instead I said. "Was *that* his name? You *knew* him? How horrible." I even shivered to show extra concern.

Maxine ignored me but sent a searing glare at Hitch. "Is that why you dropped in? To question me about my relationship with Harry? I have absolutely nothing to hide. Nothing. He dropped in and begged me to take care of his collection until he had a place of his own. End of story."

"How convenient," Hitch said. He took out his phone and snapped a photo of a gnarly twisted tree in a shallow ceramic dish. "And what are your plans for his collection now? For example... this funny looking tree that's worth... oh... several hundred thousand dollars."

"I... he... what?"

"This bonsai, Maxine. I got shot because of this plant." He rubbed his arm. "I know all about it even if you thought you could pull the wool over everyone else's eyes. Everyone except for the person who broke into Harry's well-protected apartment in New York City. The assailant got away." Hitch paused, a grim line of tension around his mouth. He looked at Maxine then back at the valuable bonsai. "And, I predict that person won't give up until this plant is removed from this new place of honor."

Maxine's face crumbled.

In one fluid motion, Hitch slipped his phone in his pocket, walked the few steps back to me and escorted me out.

"Could she be that intruder?" I asked Hitch when we were safely outside.

"Probably not, but she is about the right size. I'm thinking it's more likely she's Harry's murderer."

I paused on the walk and turned to look over my shoulder. Maxine stared at us from her big bay window.

I shivered again.

What was she up to?

9

*T*he sound of tires crunching on Maxine's gravel driveway startled me as we walked away from her house.

An old rusty sedan stopped next to Hitch's Camaro. Before I could see who was inside, he strode over to the driver's door in his casual lope. "Gina," he called out, his voice rising in his excitement. "I haven't seen you in ages. How are you?"

Gina Pitman slid out, one wrinkled pants leg followed by the other. I'd heard the young brunette who obviously spent a part of her week working out was going through some tough times. But from the dark scowl on her face, she looked like she'd just wrestled an ornery bobcat off her porch.

"I have to hurry, or I'll be late," she said breathlessly. "Mrs. Salter threatened to fire me if I'm late again. I had to drop off my friend's daughter at a new daycare facility. Poor little kid was so distraught, I couldn't just dump her and run. I've only had this job for a couple of weeks, though, and I don't know what I'll do if I get fired. And now, there's more work on my plate here with all the extra plants to take care of. I hope that guy doesn't leave them for long. He left this ugly deformed tree that's supposedly worth a fortune. I get nervous every time I walk by it." She rattled on to Hitch as though she'd seen him this morning, all the while opening the trunk and sorting out her supplies. Satisfied with her gear, she picked up a big basket filled with an assortment of cleaning supplies.

I stepped closer. "Hey, Gina. Hitch and I just got a look at all those plants. They're *your* responsibility?"

She grimaced in response.

"What's Maxine's security situation?" Hitch asked. "That has to be a huge worry." Knowing his background, I shouldn't have been surprised that he'd zero on that important detail instead of her day-to-day struggles. "With that valuable bonsai to handle, you must have her code so you can get your job done if she's gone."

"Yeah, I have the code. But she changes it every couple of days, which is a pain in the neck to keep straight." Gina slammed the trunk of her car. "Oh crap! I just locked my keys in there." She dropped her basket and buried her face in her hands as tears streamed down her cheeks. "I can't believe I just did that. Nothing is going my way lately."

"Hey," Hitch said, putting his hand on her shoulder. They'd been neighbors growing up; Gina tagging along like an annoying younger sibling Hitch had said once, before he left for New York. Apparently, their friendship was still in place. "I can pop it open for you. It'll only take a minute."

Without waiting for a reply, he headed for his car and returned with some kind of gizmo I'd never seen before. After a couple of pokes and twists, the trunk popped open, revealing a tornado of belongings. He fished around, moving shoes, clothes, and tools out of the way. "Voila! Here you go." He handed Gina her keys accompanied by a friendly pat on her back. "Try not to worry so much."

"Maxine will understand," I said, not sure at all if she would. From what I'd heard, Maxine Salter was the type of woman who insisted on having things done her way. She wasn't known for any charitable streak. My heart went out to Gina and the stress she was obviously dealing with.

"I don't think so." Gina said, confirming my suspicion about Maxine. "That's the problem. All she cares about since that guy showed up are all those orchids and that deformed tree. Whenever she looks at that ugly thing, dollar signs pop into her eyes. I can't wait for him to come back for his plants."

"He won't be back, Gina," I said softly. "He was murdered this morning. You didn't hear?"

Color drained from her face, and her mouth formed an O as big and round as her eyes. "Did it happen at the auction? Mrs. Salter said she was going to see him there and make sure he bought that nursery for his plants. She had big plans for that space."

I picked up Gina's basket of cleaning supplies and handed it to her, avoiding sharing any details about the murder. "You'd better get inside before you're late. I'm sure Maxine will figure out something to do with all those extra plants."

"Of course, she will." Gina slipped the basket handle over her arm and finger combed her tangled curls into a bit of order, then attempted to smooth the wrinkles from her uniform. "She'll keep them. Why wouldn't she?"

Gina hurried up the walkway and disappeared inside like a prisoner heading into a dungeon.

"Let's get out of here," I said to Hitch. "Before Maxine comes out and accuses us of something."

"Like what?"

"Stealing one of her special plants? I don't know, but I wouldn't put it past her to accidentally lose one and blame you for hiding it under your shirt while we were inside. It would keep any focus away from her."

Hitch, his jaw working overtime, started his car with a roar, and the tires scattered gravel as he left the driveway. My head slapped back against the headrest but the more miles between us and Maxine the better.

"Do you think Maxine and Harry were arguing about the fact that he didn't buy the nursery?" I said, replaying Gina's conversation in my mind.

"The nursery that *we* own." His face finally relaxed into a grin. "*That* will be our way in with Maxine. We'll consult with her about how to remodel that glass greenhouse to best suit my orchids. Maybe we can get her to lower her guard and find out exactly what her relationship with Harry was." He patted my leg. "You're thinking like a detective, Sunny Shaw. What other little nuggets are swirling in that amazing brain of yours?"

I glanced at Hitch to see if he was teasing me. I didn't see any twitches at the corner of his mouth or eye rolls to indicate he thought I was foolish. What I saw was his face filled with a fierce determination. That trait was what I remembered and always loved about him. He never gave up until he found all the answers. And now that he'd returned to Pineville, I planned to figure it all out right alongside him.

"I'm wondering if Maxine was angry enough to murder Harry. What do you think?" I asked.

"When someone covets something belonging to someone else *nothing* would surprise me."

I didn't like that observation, but I couldn't argue with his point about human nature.

10

"*I* have an idea," I said to break the silence. We'd been on the road for a few minutes after leaving Maxine's house. "I'm hungry. We could grab a bite and discuss our new business." I twisted in my seat to face him. "What do you think?"

"I think, Ms. Sunshine, that you read my mind, especially about the eating part. Where do you want to go?"

"Drive through Pineville toward Misty Harbor. There's a great place called the Little Dog Diner, and it just so happens that I'm friends with the owner, Dani Mackenzie. I'll send Tilly a text to meet us there."

Hitch reached over the stick shift and took my hand. "I'd rather it was just you and me…"

"But she'll never forgive me if I don't include

her. Plus, she witnessed the argument between Harry and Maxine." What I left unsaid was that being alone with Hitch for too long was confusing my emotions. On the one hand, sitting here next to him felt like old times, but the fact that he'd left for New York expecting me to drop everything I cared about to follow him, still stung. I had to take his return and our new business arrangement one step at a time. Slow and easy so my heart didn't get broken again.

"I thought this was a working lunch about *our* business?"

"That too. How about this. I'll tell her to meet us in…" I checked the time, "an hour. That way, we can talk business before she arrives." I sent off a message and got a quick okay in reply. And, it would give me enough alone time with Hitch to think about how this business relationship with him was going to work—step one.

Hitch turned onto Oceanside Road which connected all the towns along Blueberry Bay. Glimpses of stunning Atlantic Ocean views teased us as his Camaro hugged the twists and turns. Lobster boats, sailing vessels, and pleasure boats enjoying the early summer weather dotted the waves. Seagulls soared and dipped above the bay, ever present icons searching for a tasty morsel.

"How about you tell me more about your Kitty

Castle idea?" Hitch said, interrupting my daydream of all the distant adventures beyond the horizon.

I loved that Hitch had an open mind. It also didn't hurt that he couldn't resist much of anything that walked on four legs, especially an animal in need of tender loving care.

"Okay," I said with excitement surging through me. "Picture this—a corner in the greenhouse where stray kittens and mama cats can enjoy a garden-like environment with tropical plants and climbing structures under a canopy of vines." I checked if I'd gotten Hitch's attention.

He nodded enthusiastically. "Great image, Sunny. What else?"

"Add a cat door to connect the inside to an outside enclosed area for them—a catio." Ideas bubbled out. "Inside, we can have several round tables with chairs for customers to enjoy their shakes and cakes while playing with the kittens. Oh, maybe a corner with books, too—plant and cat related books—informational and fiction." I hoped I hadn't overdone the ideas. "What do you think?"

"Cats and plants?"

My heart skipped a couple of beats. Did he think I'd lost my mind?

"I love it!" Hitch added a little whoop of excitement. "And everyone else will, too."

"And, the kittens will all be available for adoption. Only to the right home, of course."

"I knew you'd make an awesome business partner, Sunny. Once we get all our ideas finalized, we'll have to decide on a contractor. The sooner the better in my opinion, so we can dazzle Pineville with this new venture. I want to get started right away."

"About that," I said. "What about the guy we met at Tilly's house? Conrad Coleman, right? Should we give him a stab at an estimate?"

"Sure, but we need to look into his experience and get recommendations for everyone we consider."

"Tilly can get more information about him from her friend. Isn't that the best kind of recommendation?"

"Usually." Hitch slowed his car at the outskirts of Misty Harbor. Something in Hitch's answer told me that Conrad wasn't high on his list. "Where's this diner we're going to?"

Okay, no point in rushing him, I thought. "Keep going straight on Main Street," I said. "You can't miss it. White with red shutters and a tidy garden in front." I pointed to the diner when it came into view. "There, lucky us, someone just left a wide-open spot. Grab it before someone else slips in."

On the sidewalk, I stretched, inhaling the salty ocean breeze mixed with aromas coming from the diner. My mouth watered in anticipation of a lobster roll overflowing with delicate tender morsels of meat.

Hitch pulled the diner door open and waited for me to enter first. His small polite gestures were impossible to miss and weakened my resolve to keep him at arm's length.

The bustle and chatter in the diner reminded me of its popularity. "I hope we can find a seat," I said as I scanned the interior. Seeing one vacant booth, I pulled Hitch to the far end of the diner where we'd even have a bit of privacy.

I spotted Christy, one of the employees, as soon as we entered the busy restaurant. "Hey, Sunny," she said as she handed us menus. "Haven't seen you for a while. How's that big dog of yours doing?"

"Jasper? You remember her" I was impressed since I hadn't been in the diner recently.

Christy laughed. "How could I forget? She filled up the office when you arrived dripping wet and terrified. At least *that* mystery got solved."

I shuddered at the memory of my frigid swim in Blueberry Bay to escape a killer. "Jasper's fine. She's home with my two kitties who will probably run circles around her."

She pulled her order pad and pen from her apron pocket. "What can I get you or do you need a little more time?"

"Nothing to think about. I made up my mind as soon as we decided to come here for lunch. Two lobster rolls, please." I ordered for both of us, knowing Hitch wouldn't be disappointed. "And two iced teas."

"Cute place," Hitch said, after Christy picked up the menus and headed toward the kitchen. Her husband did most of the cooking. "You know the owner?"

As if on cue, Dani walked over and slid in next to me. She gave me an enthusiastic hug and a peck on my cheek. "You're a sight for sore eyes, Sunny Shaw.

"Dani, this is my friend, Ty Hitchner."

"Hitch to my friends," he said with a warm smile for Dani.

Dani stretched her arm across the table to shake Hitch's hand. "What brings you to the Little Dog Diner today?" Dani asked.

"Besides your lobster rolls?" I lowered my voice. "We wanted to get away from all the buzz surrounding the murder in Pineville.

Dani rolled her eyes in commiseration. She knew a lot about murders. "I just heard about that. You aren't involved are you?" she asked in a worried rush.

A server I didn't recognize came to our table with silverware and water and I stopped to take a big gulp. Then I said, "You won't believe it, Dani. It happened right after the auction at the Nine Pine Nursery ended. The victim had been standing next to me not long before he was killed. But I guess the good news is that Hitch and I are now the proud owners of the old nursery."

Dani's eyes widened. "Congratulations! What are your plans with the place?"

"As soon as we can, we'll get started with some remodeling. We haven't made any of this public yet, but we're planning a shake and cake shop in the building, and the attached greenhouse will be home to stray kitties for adoption plus all of Hitch's orchids." I sat back with a big satisfied grin, picturing this venture done and ready to open.

"Sounds fantastic," Dani said, and I could tell she meant it. "Will Jasper be involved?"

"Are you kidding? She's already practicing to be the chief kitty nanny. I already have two kittens, and Jasper is fantastic with them. How great is that?"

"Add Pip as a back-up nanny. My little Jack Russell terrier loves kitties." Dani's phone pinged and she took it out of her pocket, scanned it briefly and returned to the conversation. "I'm so happy for you both. Best of luck getting it all up and running quickly. I know you have the energy and focus to make anything you want become a success, Sunny.

Do you have a contractor yet?" She slid out of the booth, holding up her phone as an excuse to leave.

"We're just beginning to look. Can you recommend anyone?" Hitch asked. He turned toward me to avoid the bright sunshine coming in through the large window.

Dani blushed a little. "Well, I'd recommend my husband, Luke, in a heartbeat, but I'm not sure if he can commit to your project fulltime. I've heard about a guy, Conrad Coleman, from here in Misty Harbor who gets high praise. I don't know him personally, though. I'll see if Luke knows anything more about him. He knows everyone around Blueberry Bay."

Dani smiled down at me and I could see her joy shine through her bright eyes. I felt a surge of happiness for her. I owed her a lot and didn't want to burden her with my new issues, but she seemed to have the info we needed. "Dani, would you mind talking to Luke about our plans? I'd love to hire him," I said. "He remodeled the diner for you, right?"

Dani waved her phone at me to brush away my concerns. "He did. I wouldn't mind at all. Plus, he added an apartment on my house for my grandmother. He does great work."

Christy returned with our platters overflowing with French fries surrounding an overstuffed lobster roll. "Enjoy," she said, placing the mouthwatering food in front of us.

"Yes, enjoy your lunch," Dani said. "I've got to get back to work but keep me up to date on all the news." She leaned close to my ear. "Don't let that murder derail your plans."

As if we could control that. I thought to myself.

11

*H*itch didn't waste a second before he dug into his lobster roll with ravenous gusto.

"When's the last time you ate?" I asked, slightly taken aback by his appetite.

He grinned around a mouthful of lobster and shrugged. What else could he do without spewing food across the table? As soon as he devoured the last morsel, I heard a familiar voice. "There they are."

It shouldn't have surprised me when Tilly slid in next to me, but I wasn't expecting her entourage, too. "Sue Ellen and Conrad insisted on coming," she said, helping herself to one of my leftover fries. Is that okay?"

Like I could say no when Sue Ellen and Conrad

stood at the table staring at me. That was Tilly—doing before thinking.

"We could sit in another booth," Sue Ellen said, looking around for an open spot.

"No need for that." Hitch wiped his mouth and slid out of the booth. "You two can have this seat. I have paperwork to finish up for the nursery purchase. Sunny, do you mind catching a ride home with Tilly?"

Tilly made a face that shut down Hitch's plans. "Don't be ridiculous," she said as if he was her son and she was organizing his day for him. "You don't have to leave." Tilly squashed me into the wall to make room for Conrad.

Sue Ellen slipped by Hitch and skootched herself into his place and Conrad sat next to her instead of crowding in with Tilly and me. "We have your nursery business to discuss," Tilly said. "No time to waste getting that project underway. I told Conrad that I don't mind putting my project on the back burner so he can get started on yours. Great news, right?"

Conrad's grimace told me he wasn't fully on board with Tilly's agenda. "I don't think they've had time to make that decision, Tilly," Conrad said, politely giving Hitch and me an out of this awkward situation. "Of course, I'd love to be considered, though."

"Actually," Hitch said, looking down at the four of us sitting in the booth. "We just talked to the owner here at the Little Dog Diner, and she recommended her husband, Luke. Do you know him, Conrad?"

"As a matter of fact, I do. He does good work, but he has that blueberry farm so does he have the time for your project?"

"We're checking into that," I said. I hoped that Luke could give us the background scoop on Conrad's business practices. He seemed nice enough. And, he wasn't a complete unknown with Tilly's friend, Sue Ellen, vouching for him. But, this was an important first step for Hitch and me to make. We had to get it right, and we both had to be able to work with the contractor. I'd met Luke and knew he was a standup guy. Conrad came across as a little too smooth with his hand kissing and constant grinning. It was more than obvious that Hitch wasn't taken in by that act, but I'd keep an open mind about him.

Hitch, still standing, said, "Tilly? You'll give Sunny a ride home? I trust her not to sign any contracts without filling me in first." He grinned but also gave me a quick eyebrow raise letting me know it wasn't a joke.

"Yeah, sure." Tilly waved Hitch off. With him gone, it was three against me which felt like I was trapped in a leaky rubber raft and no bucket for bailing. I steeled myself for arm twisting arguments about Conrad's brilliant abilities. Thanks, Hitch.

Christy brought coffees and a variety of muffins to the table. "Compliments from Dani," she explained, setting the tray down.

"That Dani Mackenzie sure is a class act," Tilly said. She added sugar and cream to her coffee and chose a plump blueberry muffin. "Well, help yourselves, don't expect me to fix your coffee for you."

The way Tilly stirred her own mug, splashing some over the side, told me that she had something up her sleeve. I could wait her out, no problem. I slid a coffee over and chose a muffin covered with a thick streusel topping as I waited, the sweet aroma hard to resist.

"So, Sunny." Tilly said with quite the smirk on her face. "Sue Ellen dropped Conrad off at the auction this morning. Did you see him there?"

"Actually, no. I spent most of my time face planted on the pavement. Remember? For some reason, Jasper wasn't on her leash and greeted me rather exuberantly." I had no idea why this important unless she thought Conrad killed Harry. Hmmm, was that where this was going?

Sue Ellen picked up the conversation. "Conrad knew the dead guy really well."

Well, *that* got my attention. It was my turn to

splash coffee on the booth. Not from stirring, though. My mug slipped from my fingers, crashed, cracked, and hot black liquid streamed over the edge right onto Conrad. His crotch to be exact.

"Yee gads, that's hot!" he yelled and scooched away from the dripping mess before he was completely soaked. Sue Ellen grabbed a handful of napkins and tried to mop the spill off his pants— definitely awkward.

"I'll do it myself," he said.

Tilly jabbed me with her elbow, and I stifled a laugh.

Christy heard the commotion and rushed over with a cotton towel. "What happened?"

"I'm such a klutz, sorry. I'll do that," I said, taking over the clean-up. Of the table, not Conrad. I'm not sure why Tilly's comment shocked me so much. What difference did it make whether Conrad and Harry knew each other? But, that's the problem, I never knew where a thread of connection might lead.

Conrad glared at me. Maybe working for a clumsy woman wasn't what he wanted, after all. I suspected that Hitch would be happy. Those two had not hit it off for some unknown reason.

"Oh, no big deal. No one will notice," Tilly said, glancing at the big, dark stain on Conrad's pants. We all knew she was lying. "Now… what I was about to tell you, Sunny, is that Conrad and Maxine both knew Harry." She sat back looking very satisfied.

There had to be more. I waited.

Conrad leaned over the table, focusing on me. I braced for whatever he was about to share. Tilly and Sue Ellen must have already heard it because they busied themselves with the muffins and coffee.

"Maxine wanted Harry to buy that old nursery. In a big way. She had plans for it." He raised his eyebrows. "Are you following me?"

"Just spit it all out," I said getting annoyed with this conversation. They were all in on some secret. Why didn't they just spit it out? "Look," I said, letting my frustration with them out in a loud sigh, "Why didn't he just outbid me if he was such a rich guy?"

Conrad muffled a laugh with his arm. "Who told you that?"

I flicked my wrist dismissively. "Doesn't matter who. It's not true?"

Conrad waffled his hand back and forth. "Depends how you define rich. He didn't have access to enough money to beat your bid *and* do the renovations. Anyway, that's beside the point. He didn't really want that nursery. Maxine wanted it, and now you own it with your friend. That's a big problem for her."

Little hairs on my neck shot to attention. "You think she'll come after us?" I reached for Tilly's hand under the table. Tilly, my guardian grannie who always had my back.

Then, I heard the tiniest mew. "What's that?"

"I almost forgot." Tilly pulled Stash out of her pocket. "This girl loves a cozy pocket, but maybe she wants to know what's going on. Here." She handed the magic ball of fur to me and my stress vanished. "Don't worry, Sunny. We'll protect you." I quickly glanced around to be sure no one saw the kitten and made a complaint.

In that moment, holding Stash and sitting next to Tilly, I knew I'd figure out this puzzle and come out stronger for it.

"So… Maxine?" I met Conrad's gaze with a new resolve. "She argued with Harry after the auction. Did she kill him?"

"That's the million-dollar question, isn't it?" Conrad said, leaning back against the red seat. "That's what we have to figure out."

"But you were there, too, Conrad. Maybe *you* killed your friend. Someone tried to steal his valuable bonsai plant. How many people knew about it or even had the means to gain access to his New York City apartment?"

If I hadn't been watching so closely, I would have missed the dark shadow that flickered in his eyes. I'd hit a nerve. Conrad Coleman knew more than he'd revealed so far. I made a decision that Hitch might not like, but I'd worry about that later.

"Conrad, let's discuss the remodeling we need for our new business, shall we? Tomorrow morning?" I smiled at him. When our eyes met, it felt like we were locked in a battle. For what? Information that led to a murderer?

I hoped I didn't regret this decision.

12

When I rolled out of bed Tuesday morning and my feet hit the floor, sharp pins stabbed into my ankles.

"Hey!" I shouted, leaping back on the bed. With my feet out of range, my two kittens tumbled together instead of digging their claws into my skin. They rolled around like one fluff ball with two tails and eight legs.

Poor Jasper watched from the doorway, whining pitifully. Her chocolate eyes drooped as she watched the fun.

I laughed at their antics and jumped over the kittens.

"Come on, Jasper. Don't worry about those two, we'll leave them here to dust the floor while we get some breakfast. I've got a lot of business to deal with today."

Jasper headed straight to the door letting me know that she had her own business to take care of first.

"You need to go out?" Her tail fanned in reply. "Okay, fresh air and exercise before breakfast. That works for me, too."

I filled bowls with crunchies for the kittens, pulled on my sneakers, and snapped on Jasper's leash. The leash, strictly for appearances sake, let people who saw my big companion as an intimidating menace think she was under control. Right! With Jasper outweighing me, I couldn't stop her if she made up her mind to take off.

"Sunny!" I heard Tilly shout as soon as my feet hit the pavement outside. "Wait a minute," she called as she hustled to catch up to us. She glowed in her favorite lime green jogging outfit, and with the strong morning sun, I should have worn my sunglasses to shield myself from the glaring vision. She insisted that when she was color coordinated with her car, it gave her an in-charge image. Maybe, but I had my doubts.

"Are you meeting Conrad this morning?" She handed me an energy bar and pumped her arms in sync with her pace.

"That's the plan." I picked up speed to keep

Jasper away from my neighbor's prize flower bed next to the sidewalk. I didn't see Violet peeking out her window, but that didn't mean she wasn't watching us. She had a fifth sense that told her exactly when Jasper was within ten feet of her precious blooms.

Jasper stopped, sniffed at the edge of the garden, and then wagged her tail. She looked at me with her tongue hanging out and what seemed to be a smile across her open mouth. I think she was telling me that she was having a bit of fun and not to worry. We moved on. I sighed and bit into my energy bar.

"Did you tell Hitch that Conrad is meeting you at the nursery?" Tilly asked.

Honestly, I hadn't let myself go down that path yet. Personally, I was okay with hearing his proposal, but the tension between Conrad and Hitch was a tad more than subtle. Whatever the trouble was between the two of them, I didn't want it affecting our business.

"Maybe I should cancel," I said to Tilly. We turned at the corner where a path took us through more dog-friendly terrain. I relaxed my tight hold on the leash, giving Jasper more slack and she began to sniff around.

"The way I see it," Tilly said, "no harm in hearing the guy out. Sue Ellen vouches for him.

Says he does great work. Why are you having second thoughts?"

I kicked a small rock along in front of me. "Didn't you feel the tension when Hitch first met Conrad? He doesn't like the guy, and I trust his instincts."

Tilly pulled me to a stop and forced me to look at her. "You know I love Hitch, but he doesn't trust *anyone* when he first meets them. It's his nature. He's suspicious before he lets his guard down. I'm not saying it's a bad thing, but you have to follow your *own* instincts, Sunny. Otherwise, he'll be running the show at your new business. This is the first test. Take charge of it."

Tilly had a point. I tightened the elastic on the end of my braid. "Tell me something," I said, wanting an answer to a question that had been bugging me since the whole auction thing went down. "Why does Hitch want me as his business partner? He could do it on his own and hire help."

Tilly stopped in the middle of the path. "You have to ask?" She shook her head like the answer was too obvious for words.

"Indulge me." I needed to know.

"Okay, Sunny. Here's the thing that everyone seems to see but you. Listen carefully. You're smart, hard-working, clever, and once you make up your mind, you never quit." Tilly emphasized each point with a raised finger. "Oh, and did I say having a free supply of your cakes should be number one on the list?"

"Hitch told you all that?" I was feeling embarrassed from all the compliments. Just a little, though. Who doesn't like to hear some praise once in a while?

"Honey? He doesn't have to tell me what I already know. You have to act like *you're* in charge, and then everything will fall into place."

I wished it was that easy. Nothing ever fell into place in my experience. At least not before lots of other problems were dealt with first.

We rounded the last leg of our walk. Unexpectedly, I saw Gina pacing back and forth in front of my house with her phone glued to her ear. Determination or frustration lined her face. It was hard to tell the difference.

She looked up. "Oh, thank goodness. I didn't know where else to look for you," she said with an urgency that piqued my curiosity. She tucked her phone in her bag.

"Gina? What's wrong?" I felt Tilly look at me, but she held her tongue.

Jasper pulled loose from my grip and charged toward the distraught woman.

Gina bent down to my girl. "Hello, there. I bet you don't have a mean bone in that giant body of yours, do you?" She cradled Jasper's head with both hands as she spoke, relaxing slightly from the distraction.

"I can tell that you know dogs," I said as Jasper lapped up all the attention.

"Yeah, I wish I lived in a place where I could have my own. Someday," she said wistfully. "Listen. I heard Maxine say that you bought that old nursery. Can I put in a job application?"

"Did Maxine fire you?" Jasper sat and leaned against Gina's leg. She braced herself just in time before getting knocked over from the sudden weight.

With fidgety hands, she smoothed her uniform. "No. Not yet but the stress of worrying when she will is killing me. I'd like to know I have an escape plan."

Tilly put her arm around Gina's shoulder. "Is it really that bad? I know Maxine is, well, difficult, but you have a stellar reputation."

"It's all the other things in my life right now. I've been late a few times, and she read me the riot act about it."

Gina had such a look of abject terror on her face that I had to put my arm around her too, for fear she'd break out in tears. "Gina, I'll keep you in mind, but Hitch and I haven't even finalized our business plans yet. I don't know when we'll be hiring any help." I wanted to add, I'd love to hire you, but again, this was a decision that both Hitch and I needed to make together.

I pulled away and her face fell like a deflating balloon. "You and Hitch are partners? I didn't know that. Not that it makes a difference," she quickly added. "I just thought... oh, never mind, it doesn't matter. I have to get to work. Those plants don't water themselves." She started to walk toward her car. In addition to her other problems, it looked like it was on its last legs.

"Gina. Wait," I shouted to her back.

She stopped and turned around, not looking much better.

"Do you know a Conrad Coleman? I heard he's Maxine's friend."

"Oh yeah. I see him a lot. Maxine always brings him into the plant conservatory when he visits. As a matter of fact, he came a couple of days ago, right after I got to work, with a big box of chocolates for Maxine." Gina held up her hands to show the size. "Of course, Maxine said she couldn't possibly eat any, and then she devoured four." Gina rolled her eyes.

She looked at me, then at Tilly like she wasn't sure she should continue. She stepped closer to us and lowered her voice. "Don't hold this against me."

"Of course not." My heart pounded with anticipation.

"When I'm watering and dusting, Maxine treats me like I'm invisible. I suppose her guests do, too. So, while she sits and chats and stuffs her face with chocolate, it's impossible not to pay attention. When Conrad was there, it sounded like they were planning something."

"Like what? Planning something could mean anything from a surprise party to —"

"Well," Gina interrupted, "they mentioned that guy Harry like he was already out of the picture. It made my ears really perk up. They were discussing what to do with his plants." She glanced at her wrist like she was checking the time. "Oh, right, I forgot my watch. I've got to go."

She drove off with squealing tires, a cloud of blue smoke from her exhaust, and unanswered questions swirling in my head.

I looked at Tilly. "Hitch's instinct about Conrad was right after all," I said, glad that it meant *I* was right, too.

"Maybe," Tilly said. "But it still doesn't hurt to hear his proposal."

She had a good point. Plus, we could pick his brain.

13

I parked next to Hitch's Camaro and spotted a group gathering in the far corner of the parking lot. No surprise there. The state police hovered over the spot where Harry's body was found.

Officer Walker, sneering and swaggering as usual, made his way to our car.

"What are you two up to?" he said in a tone that grated on my nerves. His stance said he was expecting an argument. Maybe, even eager for one. Even with a toothpick in his mouth, he managed to sip from his cardboard cup of coffee, eyeing me as if I were a criminal or something.

"Morning, Mick," I said as Hitch and I got out of our cars. Somehow I dredged up a friendly tone.

I hoped it threw him off his game enough to get the upper hand. I slung my bag over my shoulder ready for business.

"Maybe you forgot, but Hitch and I own this property now."

Jasper sniffed around, oblivious to my conversation.

"Yup," Hitch said with a smirk he reserved for people on his do-not-like list. "The papers are all signed and filed, so," he spread his arms wide, "here we are, ready to get to work."

"Did you clear it with them?" Mick nodded toward the state police with a less than approving gesture.

Hitch shot him a victory smile. "Sure did. So, if you don't mind," Hitch pushed past Mick, "You can find Sunny and me inside discussing our plans for Shakes and Cakes."

I walked right past Mick, ignoring his icy glare, and followed Hitch. Mick's expression hid nothing. I knew he was furious to be on the outside of the investigation looking in. Served him right. He'd been removed as the chief bully in Pineville. But he'd still try to make trouble. I was sure of that.

"What do you think?" Hitch asked as soon as we walked inside our new building. "This will work, right?"

I walked slowly around the interior, checking empty display racks and built-in shelves. I wiped my finger over the scuffs and scratches in the wooden oak counter.

"Hmm," I agreed, wiping a layer of dust off my hands on a clean-ish rag I found under the counter. "Nothing a good sanding couldn't bring back to life. Same with the wood floor."

All in all, Hitch was right. This building had plenty of space for a food prep area and several table and chair groupings.

"Conrad is stopping by to hear our needs for remodeling," I said without looking at Hitch. I needed him to know this *before* Conrad showed up.

Hitch found a couple of stools and made himself comfortable at the counter. "Perfect," he said with a twinkle stirring in his green eyes.

"You aren't going to argue with me about this?" His reaction stunned me, to say the least. Or was it a lack of reaction? I paced up and down to work off my confusion.

"Well, the way I see it," he said. He propped his elbows on the counter as if he had to brace himself for his explanation. "Since Conrad and Maxine are friends, and Maxine wanted Harry to buy this place, they'd already discussed possible renovations. We'd be stupid not to piggyback on their ideas. It doesn't mean we have to hire him, though. I just want us to be clear on that."

"Okay," I said warily. I got the warning, but I stared at Hitch wondering if he was toying with me and would have a good laugh at my expense.

"But you can't stand the guy," I stuttered.

"Sit down, Sunny." He patted the stool next to him. "You're absolutely right about my feelings for that guy. Something just doesn't feel right, but that's no reason to avoid him. I think it's much smarter to keep someone like Conrad close so we can keep an eye on him until we figure out what he's up to."

Hitch inched the stool a bit closer to me. I took the hint and sat down and gave him my full attention. "Gina was at my house this morning," I said.

He swiveled to face me. His knees bumped my thigh, distracting me. "Is that a fact? And what did she want?"

I pulled myself away from his intense gaze and said, "A job."

Now, a big deep belly laugh filled the building, bouncing around the mostly empty space.

"Sorry." He wiped his eyes as he got his laugh under control. "I suppose it's not a laughing matter to Gina, but we don't even have a business yet. What kind of job does she think we can offer her?"

"It's her backup plan. The more interesting part of our conversation was about Maxine and Conrad."

"Oh? Did she hear something while she was working?" Hitch leaned toward me, completely focused.

"She told me that she heard them discussing what to do with Harry's plants... a couple of days ago... like he was already out of the picture *before* he was murdered. Those two are up to something."

Hitch smiled and patted my knee. "I knew we'd make the best team, Sunny."

Was he talking about business partners or working together on this murder investigation? I was about to ask when a tiny *mew-mew* sound pulled my attention to the far corner of the building.

"More kitties?" My heart raced as I jumped off the stool. I stopped to listen, then tip-toed closer with each pathetic cry.

I felt Hitch's warm hand on my back as he followed right behind me until we reached the corner. No kitties and no more mews. I looked at Hitch, confused and worried.

"What now?" I asked, hoping he had a good idea. Because I had nothing.

He crouched on the floor and reached under a built-in shelf, sweeping his hand from side to side. When he looked up at me, he shook his head, and my heart plummeted.

Then scratching sounded in the back of the cabinet. Hitch had checked there, but he tried again, stretching to the very back. "Ahhh," he said, and pulled a piece of molding loose.

"I feel something moving behind this."

I could see his arm tremble and then he pulled back. "Ouch, it bit me."

He laughed and four kittens tumbled out. Four chubby soft balls of fluff mewed and blinked in the bright light shining through a window.

"Oh, Hitch, this is a sign." I jumped up and searched the space until I found a basket lying nearby. I raced back to Hitch who was trying to corral the kitties. One by one he rescued them from climbing up to his shoulders and placed them in the basket. Now down on his hands and knees, Hitch stuck his head inside the opening. I heard a muffled chuckle before he stood up and brushed his hands off.

"Clever kitties. Come and take a look."

I started to crouch down but he pulled me away from that spot and through the glass door that led into the greenhouse. I followed him to a corner where he carefully moved some pots and dead plants to one side. Someone had made a cozy nest out of an old sweatshirt. Mama cat, ignoring us, reaching into a hole with one paw.

I rushed back for the basket of kittens. As soon

as I placed it in her protected corner, she sniffed, then licked each kitty. Satisfied that they were all safe and sound, she climbed into the basket with her family and settled around them.

My hand covered my heart at this tender show of motherly love.

"Maybe your Kitty Castle should be the first project on our agenda, Sunny." Hitch's smile filled me with a new respect for this passionate friend of mine. Anyone who put animals, especially ones in need, ahead of his own agenda, was a keeper.

Without thinking, I stretched on my tippy toes, put a hand on each side of his face, and kissed him. It was a spontaneous act of thanks.

"These kitties are the sign that we're on the right path," I said.

Hitch pulled me close. "I love how you think." His voice, low and filled with passion, filled me with worry.

"Sunny?" Conrad's deep voice called.

I pulled away from Hitch, thankful for the interruption.

Conrad peeked around the glass door. "Oh, there you two are. We brought coffee and doughnuts." He held up a bag from A Donut a Day, the local donut shop with the best donuts anywhere, in my opinion.

We? I silently sent my question to Hitch, and he answered with raised eyebrows.

Maxine appeared behind Conrad. Like the day before, every hair was in place, and her cream jacket and pants reeked of money.

This was an interesting development. I thought. Why were they *both* here?

14

*H*itch placed his hand on the small of my back and gently pushed me forward. "Smile, Sunshine," he whispered. "If we want information, we need them to be nice and relaxed."

"Maxine, it's great to see you again," Hitch said, walking around me and giving her a peck on her cheek. "I apologize for my behavior yesterday. Forgive me?"

I almost choked at his performance but smiled instead, not that Maxine even made a cursory glance in my direction. I understood what Gina said about feeling invisible around her.

"Seeing Harry's bonsai in your house threw me for a loop." Hitch took her arm and led her to the stool at the counter. "You know I worked for him, don't you?"

"Yes," Maxine answered, her eyes flitting from corner to corner. "As a matter of fact, Harry asked me if I knew you, seeing as you and I are from the same town. I gave you a stellar recommendation," She waved her hand around our new building like the queen from her balcony.

"Anyway, apology accepted… *if* you agree to let me have our annual orchid society meeting here. It's perfect!"

"We're turning this space into a Shakes and Cakes Shop," I said before Maxine had any more time to woo Hitch to her plan. She could play her flirty game with him all she wanted, but she had to deal with me, too. And now was as good a time as any to let her understand that she couldn't just waltz in and ignore me.

She twitched one eyebrow up. "Sounds quaint."

I didn't expect her to be a regular patron after that polite insult. No loss.

Hitch moved swiftly, pulling two stools up to the counter so we could join Maxine and Conrad. He even managed to send me a conspiratorial wink behind her back.

Conrad slid the coffees across to us then opened his bag of pastries. A sweet aroma wafted straight to my salivary glands. My favorite—cinnamon and sugar-coated donut holes—practically jumped into my mouth.

"You were saying?" he asked as he handed me a napkin with two of the delicious treats. "About your plans?"

Maxine scowled and clenched her jaw. Apparently losing the center of attention seemed to give her indigestion.

"We can discuss the Orchid Society's needs later," Hitch said with a diplomatic nod toward Maxine. "First, we have to get our business up and running."

"And, at the top of our list is building our Kitty Castle," I said.

As if on cue, Jasper walked in carrying the tiniest of the four kittens gently by the nape of its neck. She placed the kitten on Maxine's lap. Was Jasper testing these newcomers?

She jerked backwards, yelping, "What are you doing?" as she almost slid off the stool.

Conrad reacted quickly, saving the kitten from a hard tumble. I hid a chuckle noting he saved the tiny ball of fur and not Maxine, sitting right next to him. She barely managed to catch herself, while Jasper and Conrad aced the animal rescue test with flying colors, but Maxine? Maybe she'd get a make-up exam.

"Thank you, Jasper," I said. "Are the other kitties all right?"

"There's more?" Maxine's face turned to disgust.

"Are there rats and skunks living in here, too?" She stood up and flicked a kitten hair off her jacket.

"Hitch, call me when this place is cleaned up, and I *might* still be interested. Are you coming, Conrad?"

Conrad, with the kitten cradled in his big hand, shook his head. "You go on ahead. I'll meet up with you later."

Like a pouty two-year-old, Maxine stomped her foot. "We had an agreement, Conrad."

"And I have a commitment right here. I promised my services. If I can help remodel this place and make a spot for Harry's plants, that's my goal. I thought it was yours, too, Maxine. We owe it to him."

I can't be sure, but I thought I saw smoke coming out of Maxine's ears. "I don't owe him anything," she sniffed. "Don't bother coming back to my house." She flicked her head and stalked off toward the door. Unfortunately, with her nose in the air, she didn't see the rake lying in the path and when she stepped on the handle, her sandal slipped, her ankle rolled to one side, her arms flew in the air, and she landed quite inelegantly in a pile of dirt.

I pinched my lips together, not daring to look at Hitch or I'd completely lose the tiny bit of control I managed to muster at the moment.

Meanwhile, Jasper's Newfie rescue instincts

kicked in, and she trotted over to Maxine and gave her a couple of nudges with her big head. When Maxine didn't move, she swiped her arm with her paw.

Maxine scuttled back as if Jasper had the plague. "Get off me, you big slobbery mutt." She held her manicured hand up to protect her face, but Jasper pawed through that weak defense and doubled down, licking most of blush off her face.

Hitch went to Maxine's rescue, pulling her to her feet like a knight in shining armor. But not in time to save her cream-colored outfit from Jasper's drool and black hair.

Maxine stomped out without a thank you, and Hitch and I giggled at the big dark smudge marring the back of her perfectly creased slacks.

Once her car door slammed, all my pent-up laughter let loose. Mean probably, but it felt good. People who didn't like animals didn't deserve my respect.

I finally looked at Hitch, giving me the stink eye. His giant snort mixed with my laughter and poor Conrad was lost for two minutes, sitting on his stool, still holding the tiny kitten while Hitch and I tried to get our professional act together.

I saw him looking at us and from his expression, I was sure he'd never want to work for the two of us after this performance.

Then he laughed, too. "Who doesn't love kittens?" he asked. "Where are the others?"

Jasper wagged her fluffy tail and led the way into the greenhouse to her newest charges. When we peered over the edge of her hiding spot, Mama Cat stood and stretched as if to say, *Thanks, I need a break.*

Conrad tenderly placed the tiny kitten in the basket. "Did she wander off?" he asked as he stroked Mama Cat's head. She purred her thanks and he murmured in approval. "Now I understand your Kitty Castle project," he said, with a satisfied smile lighting his round face. He looked around the greenhouse at dead plants, broken pots, and a few missing glass panes above us. "This family is in urgent need of an upgrade. What's your plan?"

I hated to admit it, but I was starting to like Conrad. I couldn't say the same about Hitch based on his stern expression. He didn't seem swayed by the appeal of the feline charm. Yet.

"What I'm thinking," I said, "is to turn that far end of the greenhouse into an enclosed garden with tropical plants and climbing structures for the kittens. A fountain might be nice, too. Eventually, once the Shakes and Cakes Shop is up and running out front, we can add tables and chairs for customers. The ultimate goal is to find homes for the kittens. Good homes," I added, thinking I'd never let someone like Maxine adopt one of our fur babies. Just talking about our plans got me excited.

Conrad turned in a full circle, his mouth silently moving. He stopped. "And the rest of the greenhouse?"

"For my orchid collection," Hitch said. "Well, orchids and other specialty plants for sale."

Conrad nodded slowly. "Maxine will approve of that, but she obviously wasn't a fan of the Kitty Castle."

I bristled with anger. Who did she think she was? "We don't need her permission. *We* own this property."

"Sorry. That didn't come out the right way. I was only making an observation. I know what Maxine hoped for if Harry bought this place. I don't think she's really come to terms that she's out of the picture."

"Is that why she came with you today?" I asked. "She thought she could flutter her eyelashes at Hitch." I fluttered mine for emphasis. "And twist him around her little finger to do her bidding?"

That woman was really under my skin now. Maybe she thought because she had every hair in place and wore designer clothes, sadly stained, right now I reminded myself happily, she thought she could have anything and everything she wanted

with a snap of her fingers, including Harry's valuable bonsai.

Hitch stacked some empty pots as he casually
walked around our greenhouse. Part of his appeal
was his easy manner and the way he made himself at
home even in our dusty fixer-upper. Also, the way
he always got right to the point.

"Maxine and Harry were arguing before he was
murdered." Hitch directed this statement at Conrad.
"Was it about Sunny buying the property instead of
Harry?"

Leave it to Hitch to dig around for the important
information.

"Probably," Conrad said. "She was fuming mad
when I saw her. Her housekeeper had just asked me
where she could find Maxine, but she looked petri-
fied to approach her. Gina, is that her name?"

"Gina was at the auction?" As soon as the question left my mouth, I knew it was kind of silly. Of
course, Gina was there if Conrad had spoken to her.

"Yeah, she said she needed the new code for the
security system in case Maxine wasn't there to let
her in. She said something about helping a friend
with her kid, and she didn't want to be late." He
shrugged like it didn't make much sense to him. "I
guess Maxine trusts Gina."

Hitch glared at Conrad with what seemed to me
to be unnecessary aggression. "Does she trust *you*?"

I didn't know what had gotten into him.

"Who the heck *are* you?" Hitch stepped closer. His voice held an undertone of quiet rage only I would notice.

Conrad's mouth opened and closed soundlessly.

"Let me make a wild guess," Hitch sneered. "You were in New York a couple of months ago... at Harry's apartment... at the same time I was there." Hitch lifted his injured arm. "I wish Harry, your friend, was a better shot and hit *you* instead of me."

The color drained from Conrad's face. "I can explain."

"I bet you can, but who's going to believe you?" Hitch pointed to the door. "We aren't interested in doing business with you."

Conrad didn't deny Hitch's accusation. I think the color must have drained from my face, too, at what *that* implied.

Conrad had already tried to steal Harry's valuable bonsai plant once?

What was he planning next?

15

"*H*itch?" I touched his arm with my fingertip. "I don't understand what just happened with Conrad."

His shoulders slumped, and he rubbed his injured arm. "I don't understand everything either, but now that I know who the intruder in Harry's apartment was, I've got one piece of the puzzle. It might mean that we're closer to the center of this mess."

Jasper leaned against Hitch with her head tipped up in her I-know-something's-wrong pose. He stroked her soft fur. She was a hard act to ignore but so incredibly easy to love.

"I've got an idea," I said.

I double-checked Mama Cat and her kittens. When I was sure they sure all were accounted for, I left their secret hidey-hole open in case they wanted a dark hiding spot, found a plastic bowl, and turned on the greenhouse hose. Water gushed into the bowl. That was a relief at least.

I tightened up everything as much as possible and scratched her adorable head. She mewed when I told her, "I'll bring you back some tasty crunchies." Did she understand I was trying to help? I hoped so. At any rate, it was all I could do for the moment.

Hitch had his folder of papers gathered together when I returned to the main building.

"Let's go back to my house to discuss our plans without more interruptions. What do you think?" I asked, hoping I sounded upbeat and positive.

Hitch nodded. "I'm sorry I was rude to Maxine and Conrad. That wasn't my plan, but once I figured out that Conrad was the intruder in Harry's apartment, I guess I went a little crazy." He smiled reassuringly. "Still want to be my partner?"

"You can't get rid of me that easily, Hitch. We're in this together—with thick shakes, sweet cakes, cuddly kitties, and outrageous orchids."

"Darn." His eyes creased at the edges letting me know he was teasing. "When you put it that way, I guess we have to make it work one way or another." He gave me a friendly pat on the shoulder. "Let's go, then."

Jasper and I led the way to my house. As excited as I was for this new business adventure, at the moment, I was glad to return to the safety and security of my own space. I let out a deep exhale when I opened the front door. The steady tick-tock of my favorite wall clock and the familiar scent of pine candles was what I needed. But where were the kittens who should be greeting me with a sneak attack?

Jasper ran inside, her deep angry bark shaking my little house. Everything, as far as I could tell in that instance, seemed normal. Yet, she sensed something was wrong.

"Stay by the door, Sunny," Hitch said, rushing by me. His hand reached for his holster under his denim jacket, and he followed Jasper into my kitchen.

His reaction shot fear straight to my pounding heart.

"What are *you* doing here?" Hitch's voice demanded.

Who was he talking to? I wasn't going to hide in the corner when some unknown person was in my house. I charged forward, ready for anything. Or, so I thought.

"Gina?" *I was ready for anything but Gina.* "What *are* you doing here? And how did you get inside?"

She quickly glanced with a hollow-eyed expression at Jasper's dog door, still brushing grit from her hands. Right. Wasn't that how I'd planned to break into my own house the day before? I needed to get a lock for that thing.

"You need to lock that dog door," Hitch said as if I hadn't already figured that problem out myself.

I jabbed Gina's chest with my pointer finger. "What happened to my kittens?"

She had such a frightened expression, I regretted my aggressive move, but I needed answers. "I tried to stop them. Really, I did. But they squeezed out while I was squirming in."

Jasper, forever the perfect nanny, pushed through her dog door into the backyard. I followed but took the more grown-up path—the door.

"Sorry," I heard Gina say in a tiny scared voice. "I didn't know where else to go. I think they're framing me for Harry's murder."

"Who's framing you?" I asked, still reeling from this unwanted intrusion. My mind was on finding Stash and Princess Muffin. Both problems tore me in opposite directions.

"Maxine? Maybe with Conrad's help?"

I sighed with relief as Jasper, oblivious of the thorns, nosed under my rose bush and pulled Princess Muffin out. Stash, not to be left behind, followed and both kitties returned safely back inside after their little adventure.

With that mishap under control, I put my kettle on, got out my basket of tea, mugs, and honey, moving around on autopilot. Waiting for the next bombshell to drop.

Hitch took the basket before he turned on Gina. "That's a harsh accusation," he said, giving her an opening to explain herself.

"I know, and I'm really scared. Come take a look at what's in the trunk of my car. Please?"

I looked out the window and saw her old sedan, as drab as Gina looked with her shapeless pants and t-shirt and stringy brown hair. I should have noticed the car before, but I was in too much of a rush to get in my house. So much for my powers of observation, but what was Hitch's excuse?

"Okay. Let's go," he answered.

"Should we all go? And Jasper, too?" I asked. Was a crowd safer if something was going on?

Gina paced across my kitchen. "Listen, I've been waiting here for about a half hour trying to figure out what options I have. Either come and take a look or I'm outta here."

Hitch opened the kitchen door, letting Gina lead the way. He looked at me. "Well? Are you coming?"

Of course, I was. Curiosity always got the better of me. I could no more stay inside and wonder what the mystery in Gina's car was than I could abandon those kittens.

Gina, determined now, strode out to her car, eyes straight ahead, as if oblivious to danger, and popped her trunk open. In among the litter of her life crammed around the spare tire was Harry's gnarled bonsai tree.

I gasped.

"You stole it?" Hitch asked. "Do you have any idea how easily you could damage that tree while it bounces around in there?" He lifted it out like it was a fragile sculpture.

"I didn't steal it! It was in there when I left work. I opened my trunk to put my basket of work supplies inside and got the shock of my life. *They* put it there. They're framing me."

No wonder she looked so frazzled. "Why?" I asked, feeling like this whole situation only got crazier with each passing minute. "Hitch told me that plant is worth a fortune, and someone tried to kill him while he was protecting it. Why would they frame you, Gina?"

She looked at me like I had two heads or four eyes or some other alien feature sprouting out of my head. "Because *they* killed that guy, and they need the police to look elsewhere. Who am I? Just a struggling young woman trying to make ends meet cleaning up after all the rich people in town who treat me like I don't even exist. Maxine has all the connections. I don't." She slammed the trunk closed.

"I'm leaving. You can do what you want with that thing."

"Wait!" Hitch said and lunged for Gina. But, with the bonsai cradled in his arms, she easily slipped out of reach and got in her car. Without looking back, she sped off leaving two rubber burns on the tar.

"What now?" I asked.

A siren sounded in the distance, getting louder with each pound of my heartbeat. I looked at Hitch.

"This isn't good," he said.

16

My heart pounded as I listened to the siren get closer and closer. Hitch jumped into action.

Working quickly, he placed the bonsai among my rock garden plants and covered the pot with mulch and stones. I marveled at the transformation and how easily he'd hidden this valuable plant right in plain sight.

Officer Walker stopped in front of my house, got out of his SUV, and surveyed the scene, the ever-present toothpick making the rounds of his jaw

"Where's Hitchner?" he barked. "He's wanted for questioning about a breaking and entering, and theft. And don't try to lie to me, Sunny. For all I know, you two were in on this together."

"Gee, I don't see him around here, Mick," Tilly

said, jolting me with her unexpected comment as she pranced across the street.

I looked around, too. Where had Hitch disappeared to? He'd just been by my side. I'd have to wing this problem blind.

"But I'm glad you showed up when you did, Mick," Tilly said, corralling the officer. "You must have ESP or something. Someone's been stealing my hydrangea blooms when I'm asleep at night." She huffed an indignant breath before continuing. "I just can't figure it out. Come over here and take a look."

"I don't have time for that now, Tilly." Walker tried to brush her off with his most officious voice.

I choked back a snort. He didn't know Tilly.

"What are you talking about?" She shot him her best hurt expression. And, believe me, Tilly could make a rock cry if necessary. "You're the town police officer, and I'm in need of your services." She grabbed his arm and dragged him across the street.

"See?" she pointed. "Right there. Snip, snip, and more big blooms snipped right off. These luscious blue blooms were my pride and joy." She actually swiped her cheek even though I knew it was all for show since those hydrangeas were in a vase in her house.

"What are you going to do about it?"

While Tilly held Mick captive in her yard, I

snuck around to my back door. If Hitch was still around, this was his chance to book it to the next county, leaving me to clean up this mess, which I was happy to do if it kept him safe.

Whatever Conrad and Maxine were up to stunk to high heaven. Somehow, they figured that Gina would find Hitch and ditch the bonsai. It was a brilliant plan. Leave the evidence with the guy who wanted revenge for being shot.

"Pssst."

I turned around. Hitch had my kitchen door cracked open and was waving frantically for me to go inside.

"How long can Tilly keep Mick trapped by her bushes?" he asked, trying to peer around the corner of the house to gauge the action on the street.

I waved him inside before Walker spotted him. "Maybe fifteen more minutes. Are you leaving?" I squeezed passed him, and he shut the door.

"No! That would only make me look like I have something to hide."

"Like a valuable bonsai tree?"

Hitch pulled out a chair at my kitchen table and gestured for me to sit down.

"Mick doesn't know a bonsai from bamboo. No, we're going to sit here like our only concern is getting our business up and running. We have nothing whatsoever to hide, Sunny. Zero. When he finally comes in, we'll have our business plans spread out here, a pot of tea ready, and a to-do list prepared for the rest of the day."

"I don't know, Hitch." I was the worst liar in Pineville, and he knew it.

"You don't have to lie," he said, reading my mind. "Well, maybe a little when it comes to Gina's visit. Just let me handle everything. Mick is after me, not you. As far as Mick is concerned, the sun always shines on your long dark hair."

The tea kettle whistled. I jumped. Hitch took my face between his strong hands. "You can do this, Sunny. Remember, our future rides on getting past what looks like a giant frame-up. Gina was right about one thing, but the target wasn't her. It's me."

I nodded, gritted my teeth, and dug deep within for the strength I'd need.

Hitch filled my teapot and brought it to the table.

"One thing, Hitch. How did you know it was Conrad that tried to steal Harry's bonsai in New York?"

He sat down opposite me. "The one image that was burned on my brain was that the intruder wore white sneakers. Not just any white sneakers. His had a partial red heart with eyes on the side. Unforgettable. And, do you know where I saw those same sneakers? On Conrad's feet. At first, I wasn't positive, but, this morning in the greenhouse, I decided I had nothing to lose by calling him out."

"But the intruder had a mask on," I said. I found it hard to believe that someone I'd sat next to was a potential thief and possibly a murderer.

Hitch took both my hands in his. "Sunny, Conrad didn't deny my accusation, did he?"

I shook my head. Hitch was right about that and all it meant. "So, what are we going to do?" I took a deep breath because I could feel panic rising inside me again.

Hitch poured me a cup of tea. "Have some. It's an herbal mixture that's supposed to calm stress. We're going to plan our business like nothing's out of the ordinary. When Mick comes in, we'll smile and throw a couple of insults like we always do, but we aren't going to give him any reason to think we know a thing about the missing bonsai tree. He's got nothing. Remember, we were at the greenhouse, and then we came here. We didn't have time to steal that plant even if we wanted to."

"Okay. That all makes sense. I can do this." Saying it out loud helped me think it was possible. Wasn't everything just mind over matter anyway? We didn't steal the plant, so that's what I had to focus on. Plus, I didn't want to rat on Gina and put her in the crosshairs. I felt better already, and I hadn't even taken a sip of tea.

Until a loud knock sounded on my front door.

Hitch put his hand on my knee. "This is it, Sunny. You okay?"

I nodded and walked to the door. Jasper woofed loud enough to scare the kittens, sending them skittering into a safe hiding spot under the couch. That was normal and comforting. And, Mick was a bully I reminded myself. I stood tall and opened the door.

"Can I come in, Sunny?"

I was prepared to see Mick standing there. But, Tilly? I almost cracked up at the sight of her behind him with her palms up and shoulders scrunched. I had to look away.

"Who's there, Sunshine?" I felt Hitch behind me and saw a dark cloud pass over Mick's face. He'd always hated my friendship with Hitch. Hearing that pet nickname probably threw him over the edge with jealousy.

"Officer Walker, did the state police send you on an errand?" Hitch asked, turning the knife a full twist at Mick's demotion.

Mick's eyes were a glowing pit of fury.

He smiled, but it certainly didn't reach those angry eyes.

"I have my own case, and I have some questions for you, Hitchner. We can do it here, or you can come to the station. Your choice."

"What do you think, Sunshine? Do you want to

invite Officer Walker inside?" Hitch gently squeezed my shoulder and sent me a shot of courage.

I held my hand out in welcome to Mick. "Okay. Come on in, Mick."

Showtime, I told myself.

Just remember what's at stake.

Everything.

17

Tilly made herself comfortable in my chair that faced the window. She insisted on having an outside view at all times to prepare for the unexpected. She said that strategy had saved her life more than once. Maybe, but she also liked to exaggerate.

Hitch and I sat on the couch, which left my wobbly-legged chair for Mick.

With great fanfare, Mick set a recorder on his thigh. "Do I have your permission to record this conversation, Mr. Hitchner?" Now that he was doing official business, he'd added the formal title.

"Yes," Hitch said.

Mick hit a button and recorded his name, date, location, and the names of everyone present.

"Mr. Hitchner," Mick said, "where were you this morning?"

I wondered if this was some kind of trick question because Mick had seen us at the greenhouse.

Hitch crossed his legs and gave Mick that laid-back easy smile. "Well, I spoke to you at the new business property Sunny and I bought yesterday, Mick. So, that's where I was."

He looked at me and rolled his eyes. In a whisper the recorder wouldn't pick up, he added. "At the rate we're going, this is going to be a long interview."

"And, before that?" Mick asked.

"My house."

"Can anyone verify that?"

"I can," Tilly said with her hand raised. "I took Hitch some muffins first thing like I do on most mornings. Otherwise, I'm afraid he won't get enough to eat. And, you know that breakfast is the most important meal of the day. Do you eat in the morning, Mick?" She cocked her head and waited for an answer.

Hitch jabbed me in the side with his elbow, which set off a giggle.

"Tilly," Mick said. "Please keep your comments to yourself. All these questions are for Mr. Hitchner."

"But, Mick," she whined, "you asked if *anyone* could verify that he was at his house. I'm that *anyone* who just verified his whereabouts."

"I was asking Mr. *Hitchner* if *he* knew of anyone who could verify that he was home. If there are any more outbursts, I'll have to ask you to leave. Understand?"

"I was only trying to help." She stuck her bottom lip out and crossed her arms. The chance that Tilly could keep quiet was about the same chance that I'd ever learn to fly.

"Tilly was right," Hitch said. "She brought me muffins. Delicious raspberry cream cheese muffins. Did you make them, Tilly?" Hitch asked.

She guffawed. "You know I don't go near the kitchen, Hitch. Except for food that doesn't need to go on the stove or in the oven."

"I'm asking the questions!" Mick said. From his tone of voice, he was getting frustrated and having trouble keeping his cool. This was all on tape, and I was positive he didn't want his superiors to hear him lose control in front of a potential witness.

I leaned back, enjoying the show immensely.

"Mr. Hitchner, did you go to Maxine Salter's home yesterday?" Again, that infuriating smile, this time directed at me.

"Yes."

"Did you take any pictures?"

"Yesterday? Yes."

"Of what?"

"I took lots of pictures of our new business property as a before memory to show customers for after we get all the renovations done."

"I meant when you were at Maxine's house. Did you take any photos when you were *in* her house?"

"I did."

"And, what did you take a picture of?"

"Actually, I took several. Mostly photos of Sunny in Maxine's beautiful conservatory. The light was perfect to accentuate her flawless skin and shiny hair." He pulled his phone out of his pocket. "Would you like to see them?"

Mick took the phone and scrolled through the photos. "Maxine said you took a picture of her bonsai tree?"

"Her bonsai tree?" Hitch looked at me with his eyebrows raised. "What's he talking about?"

I shrugged and squeaked all innocent like, "I don't know," hoping Mick didn't catch the nervous twitch starting in my eye.

Mick leaned forward and the chair wobbled, somehow reducing his authority. He sat up straighter but didn't quite recover his superior attitude. "Oh, come on, you two," he said. "Quit playing around. Maxine has a collection of plants from Harry Jenson, and she said you took a picture of the bonsai tree."

Hitch shook his head, a picture of confusion pasted on his handsome face. "Huh. I'm not sure why Maxine would have those valuable plants. Do you know how much Harry's bonsai tree is worth?" He whistled, the way men do when they're talking about something important, like cars or fish they've caught. "More than you'll make in a lifetime, Mick. Isn't it odd that those plants are in Maxine's conservatory and Harry is dead now?"

That statement hung in the air for Mick to consider. It was masterful how Hitch had twisted the whole bit about the tree away from himself and right back where it belonged—on Maxine.

Mick pushed a button on the recorder with a disgusted snap. "That's all for today." He stood up. "I'll let myself out." I didn't think that was for our convenience.

Maybe Mick's petulance was making a point. Maybe it was because things didn't go the way he had planned. Maybe Maxine had gotten his hopes up after she'd planted some concocted version of *her* story in his head. At any rate, I felt a teensy tiny bit sorry for him until he turned around at the door.

"Whatever you did with that plant, you won't get away with it," he snarled.

I mean, that bit of nastiness was uncalled for.

"Don't let the door hit you on the way out," Tilly said. She was never one to let a golden opportunity slip by. She watched through my front window and said, "The coast is clear," when he drove off.

"Now, tell me what's going on." She pointed at my rock garden. "Oh, nice new little tree you have out there, Sunny. Where'd you get it? I want one just like that."

Hitch and I both cracked up.

"That, Tilly," I said, "is the bonsai tree that poor Officer Walker is looking for. Straight out of Maxine's conservatory."

She looked at me, then at Hitch. Her mouth opened but nothing came out. I savored this rare moment when Tilly Morris's tongue was silent.

Finally, she managed to utter, "How?"

"Gina said someone planted it in her car. She didn't want anything to do with it, so she brought it here," I explained. "And now, she's gone into hiding."

"I suppose that's smart on her part," Tilly said. "The way Maxine operates, Gina is a disposable item in her tool kit. If Maxine killed Harry after that argument I witnessed, she'll do anything to divert attention to someone else. Poor Gina."

"And get Mick to do her dirty work," Hitch added.

I laughed. "She needs someone smarter than Officer Walker if she plans to take you down, Hitch. He didn't know if he was coming or going by the time he left."

"Do you think Maxine offered him a reward to find the bonsai?" Hitch asked. "That would be a clever way to get him running around looking for a needle in a haystack for her."

"Or, a tree in a garden," I said.

From Tilly's chuckle, I knew she had mischief on her mind.

"Only Maxine and Conrad would notice that bonsai for what it is, Sunny. How about we camouflage it with some pink flamingoes. If Maxine did a drive by, that sight would be too horrible for her to notice. She'd turned up her nose at the tacky pink birds."

I high-fived Tilly and she clapped her hands with delight. "I can see her face now, all puckery like an old dried apple." Tilly sucked her lips together and crossed her eyes to give me a preview. "It's a perfect idea and the best part?" Her gleeful expression was exactly Tilly at her happiest. "I have a flock of pink flamingoes in my garage."

Of course, she did. I hoped it worked because having that bonsai out in the open was asking for trouble.

The tree was the reason Hitch got shot in the arm.

The next time, the shooter might aim to kill.

This was getting too dangerous for my liking.

How would we stay safe *and* get our business going?

18

*T*illy took great pleasure in creating an artistic arrangement of her flamingo flock around the stolen bonsai tree. When she finished, the tree branches wove in and out of stick-like flamingo legs as if the flock was clustered at the water's edge. I admired her handiwork and crossed my fingers that this small effort might conceal our problem for now before I went inside.

Hitch sat at the table hovered over his tablet.

"I want to go check on the kittens and take them food, Hitch. Will you come with me?" I didn't want to admit to him that going by myself, after everything that had happened, was all a bit much for my nerves.

"I'll meet you there, okay?" he said. "Take Jasper if you're feeling a little vulnerable.

I stared at him in disbelief. "How do you do that? You always know what I'm thinking. It's not fair, Hitch. And you walk around with your stone face expression like nothing ever bothers you."

He gave my shoulder an affectionate tweak. "You just answered your own question, Sunshine. All your emotions light up your face like fireworks. That's one of your qualities that I find hard to resist."

Really? I felt my face warming. Maybe being expressive had its perks.

"All I do is hide stuff." Hitch said. "If I let one speck of concern or indecision show when I'm working as a security guard, I lose the upper hand. That could mean my life, or this."

He held up his injured arm. My stomach curled at the thought of Hitch taking a bullet.

But he just grimaced and told his story. "I should have known that Harry had a gun that night, but I let my guard down thinking I had every angle covered. Why he decided to take a shot, though, is still something I haven't figured out. If you don't want to be an open book, work on a good poker face."

"I can do that," I said, even though I knew it was a lie.

"Sunny? Say it like you mean it, even if you

don't." He grinned that dimple-filled grin, and I couldn't help but laugh.

Maybe I could learn to fool some of the people some of the time, but I'd probably never fool Hitch. He knew me too well.

I broke away from his gaze and called my favorite companion. "Come on Jasper. We've got kitties to feed."

Armed with kitty crunchies, bowls, fleece blankets, and the best nanny dog around, we drove toward my new dream. Sure, I had my doubts about making the Shakes and Cakes Shop come to life, but it was time to put Tilly's nonstop advice into action: give it your best shot and see what happens.

At least the location was perfect. After renovations, the building would buzz with customers. I was sure of that. And best of all—I had plenty of ideas.

I turned into the parking lot, happy to see I had the place to myself. The police must have bagged and tagged all the evidence they could find. Now they faced the tedious task of following the clues to find Harry's murderer.

I hoped they didn't find a link to Hitch. Deep in my gut, I knew he didn't kill Harry. An excellent shot, if he'd wanted to, he could have picked Harry off the night of the shooting, claiming self-defense. No, one thing we've learned from Harry's appearance here at the auction in Pineville, other people wanted him dead. Maxine and Conrad immediately came to mind.

Jasper jumped out as soon as I opened my car and made a beeline for the door. She whined and scratched to get in.

"What's the matter?" I asked, suddenly less confident about being here alone. The quiet rustle of leaves in the surrounding trees and cawing of crows overhead should have made me feel at peace. Instead, hairs prickled on my neck.

I opened the door, letting Jasper lead the way.

Of course, she went straight to the greenhouse and the corner where we'd left Mama Cat and her kittens.

No mews met my ears, only Jasper's nails clicking on the cement floor.

I moved the old boxes hiding her spot and peeked into an empty basket.

"Oh no, Jasper! Where did they go?"

Did Mama Cat move her family thinking we were the enemy? Jasper poked her nose around until we heard a faint mew coming from the hole. I stood breathless as a little tabby face peeked out. One kitten after another pushed through the opening and batted Jasper's nose. Mama Cat had hidden her babies while she scouted up a meal and now she returned to her charges. What a smart mama.

I crouched and gave her several strokes along the length of her body, and she rewarded me with a purr. At least, she wasn't skittish. After filling the bowls with dry food and fresh water, I sat on the floor and watched the family chow down.

"You're gonna love the new garden we've got planned for you," I said to Mama Cat. I pictured the kittens in our man-made forest instead of this dirty corner.

A man croaked, "Sunny?" breaking into my reverie. I turned to the door on a stab of fear at the sound of Conrad's voice behind me. Here I was, alone, lost in my daydream, and caught by one of the people I suspected might have killed Harry.

I gulped instead of greeting him, and instinctively reached for Jasper. I pulled her close to me, my eyes wide with questions for the intruder. Jasper hadn't growled, which made me feel slightly safer. Wouldn't she sense if Conrad planned to harm me?

"Sorry," Conrad said, coming toward me. "I didn't mean to surprise you, but I saw your car and…"

I stood up feeling less vulnerable *on* my feet instead of *at* his feet. "And what, Conrad?" Jasper leaned into my leg. At least she wasn't lapping at the intruder's hand. "Didn't Hitch make it clear that you aren't welcome here?"

Conrad ran his fingers through his thinning hair. Stubble sprouted on his face and a sadness filled his eyes. "I need your help," he said.

We stared at each other for what felt like much too long. Then, Mama Cat wove in and out between my legs, purring, and head butting me. I picked her up. "What is it, Mama Cat?"

"Mama Cat?" Conrad asked. "That's her name?"

"Well, for now."

"And the kittens? Have you named them, yet?" He squatted down and groaned a little. "These knees aren't what they used to be," he said and picked up the tiniest one that he'd rescued from falling off Maxine's lap. The one with sapphire blue eyes, rimmed by white and set in mostly gray fur, soft as down.

What was he doing with all this friendly kitty behavior? I didn't want to like this man and be disloyal to Hitch's feelings. But he seemed to really care. What would it hurt just to listen to him?

Conrad held up the kitten and grinned at it, eye to eye. "How about Razzleberry? Someone has to give you a name."

He was talking to the kitten but seemed to be waiting for a reply from me. What should I do?

Jasper woofed, breaking the tension. Both Conrad and I laughed.

"Razzleberry it is, then," I said.

"So." Conrad tucked Razzleberry between Mama Cat and my arm. "Will you help me?"

"If I can," I said brightly, even though it was a lie. Hitch's motivational speech was kicking in. I'd help Hitch in a heartbeat. This guy? Not so much.

Conrad sat on the floor and folded himself into a cross-legged position, surprising agility for his age, I thought.

I sat down, too, but kept Jasper between us. I had to find out what he wanted.

It was the least I could do to satisfy my curiosity.

I hoped I wasn't making a terrible mistake.

19

"*I*'m not the enemy," Conrad said.

He wasn't a friend, either, I told myself. What was the something in between called? Frenemy?

"I noticed how much you liked these." He handed me a waxed paper bag.

I had an unhealthy weakness for cinnamon-covered donut holes. The aroma was intoxicating, and the taste was to die for. What? Not the best thought but I popped one in my mouth anyway. I hoped this craving wasn't going to get me in trouble.

"Conrad, why do you need my help?" I mumbled around the mouthful of deliciousness. "You're the reason Hitch was shot."

While I waited for his denial or flimsy excuse about that disaster, the kittens decided that Jasper was a mountain to be conquered. They climbed over her paws and up her side, even tackled her fluffy tail. Jasper tolerated all of it. No, I think she enjoyed the attention.

Conrad ignored the kittens and said, "That was never part of the plan."

"What plan?" I looked at him, sensing there was a lot hidden behind that comment.

"Our plan," he answered as if *that* clarified anything.

"Yours and Maxine's?"

His eyebrows jumped up and he let out a harrumph.

"Listen, Conrad. I think your words were, 'I need your help.'" I was getting tired of his cat and mouse game, and my survival instinct told me to get rid of this con man.

"Okay. I'll level with you, but don't tell Hitch. Deal?"

I paused for effect before I crossed my fingers and lied right to his face. "Deal." This poker face stuff was getting easier. Hitch would be proud. I think. Or else, he'd think I'd put myself in a dangerous situation—sitting on the floor with a cat in my lap while this suspected killer I barely knew plied me with my favorite snack and got me to make a stupid promise. Where was Hitch, anyway?

Conrad leaned toward me in a time-tested

sincerity ploy. "Harry came up with a plan. I didn't want any part of it, but if I hadn't agreed, he would have found someone else. And that would have been much riskier. He could trust me."

Right. Trust me. I didn't think so. That sounded like a con man's famous last words. I nodded my head so he'd continue.

"Harry needed money," he said. "No one else knew this, but his wife was diagnosed with early onset Alzheimer's disease. He took care of her for as long as he could, but when it became impossible for him to do it alone, he found the best care money could buy. I suggested a facility in the Blueberry Bay area, and I think that's where Charlotte is."

That tugged on my heart strings. If it was true. I ate the last donut hole, found a tissue to wipe my sugary mouth, and waited for him to continue.

"In hindsight, his plan sounds terrible, but I can't go back and change what's already set in stone." He dragged his hand along the stubble on his chin and sighed deeply. "Harry wanted me to steal his bonsai tree so he could make an insurance claim."

"What?" I glared at Conrad. "Hitch got shot over an insurance scam? Are you here to finish the job? One arm wasn't enough?"

I knew I wasn't making much sense and Mama Cat scooted away when I raised my voice, but I couldn't stop my ranting rage. "Now, I suppose you're going to insist it was just an accident that he got shot."

Conrad's voice took on a pleading tone. "It *was* an accident. Harry never told me he had a gun. Let me back up. When Harry took out the insurance policy, he had to prove he had enough security to protect his assets. He installed alarms and hired Hitch to be the security guard. The gun was never part of the plan."

I shook my head to rid it of the cobwebs, or whatever was making Conrad's story so confusing. "Explain the plan, Conrad, because I'm lost except for the part about you helping Harry scam the insurance company. Why didn't he just sell the bonsai tree to the highest bidder?"

Conrad was becoming agitated, as if the memory of recent events was stirring up his feelings. "He couldn't bear to part with it. He wanted to have his cake and eat it too, which, as we all know now, didn't work."

I barked out a sardonic laugh. "And, never does. So, now what? I don't see how I can help you. I don't know who killed Harry."

"I need you to help me get the bonsai tree back."

Well, that rocked my socks. "Back? From Maxine?" I certainly wasn't going to let him know that Gina dumped it on me and ran.

"I took it out of Maxine's house while she was getting her hair done. She's a creature of routine so I looked at her calendar and picked the best opportunity. I acted on impulse because I was afraid she'd contacted a buyer."

"You took the bonsai tree and now you don't know where it is? Come on, Conrad, I wasn't born yesterday."

"I didn't time it all very well. Maxine came back sooner than I expected, and I didn't have time to put it in my car, so I put it in the trunk of Gina's car. I don't want her to find it before I retrieve it."

Ha, too late for that. What kind of thief was this guy? "The solution sounds simple enough. Take it out of Gina's car when she shows up for work. You don't need *my* help for that, Conrad."

Did he have an ulterior motive to find out what I knew? Was he framing Gina like she suspected? "What are you really doing here?"

"There is the possibility that Gina already found the plant and has it hidden somewhere. You know Gina. Maybe you can talk to her. That's all. Just see if you can find out anything."

"You seemed obsessed with that bonsai tree. Why? With Harry dead, are you planning to sell it and keep the money?"

Conrad bristled at my question. I'd hit a nerve, and he didn't like it. Jasper shifted closer to me, and

I saw Conrad's hand slip inside his jacket. Was he going to shoot me?

"Here." He handed me a business card. "Call me if you learn anything. The bonsai tree belongs to Harry's wife, and the least I can do is save it for *her*. It will provide money for her care. Like I told you already, Sunny, I'm not the enemy. Think about what I've told you. I trust you'll do the right thing."

Well, he shouldn't trust me. I'd do what I thought was right and that most likely wouldn't line up with his wishes.

Conrad patted Jasper and stood up. "Nice dog you have. Good luck with your Kitty Castle. I'd love to help if Hitch changes his mind."

He walked away, shoulders sagging, and his hands hanging limp at his sides.

I wish I knew what to believe.

Between Conrad, Gina, and Maxine, there was enough confusion to keep me guessing for the rest of the year.

20

*H*itch arrived while I was still sitting on the floor with Jasper, Mama Cat, and the kittens. I'd tried to make sense of everything Conrad told me, but the question remained. Did I believe he was telling the truth? I just didn't know.

"Hey, Sunshine." Hitch strode across the floor like he owned the place. Which he actually did. He hunkered down next to me and said, "I see you're busy working." He ruffled my hair, something he'd been doing since we were kids. I twisted away, never liking that gesture that made me feel like a child.

"Hitch?"

He sat down next to me and cuddled one of the kittens. "What's on your mind?" he said cheerfully. Somehow, he always managed to keep a positive outlook during this catastrophe. Something I failed at. Miserably.

I had plenty on my mind, but I wasn't sure I wanted to jump in headfirst.

So, I deflected. "Do you have a plan for the renovations?" I asked. That was a safe enough topic. "I mean, you threw out the one contractor who had time in his schedule to start right now."

One of the kittens tried to crawl up on his knee, and he tickled it under its scruff. "How about your friend, Dani Mackenzie's husband over in Misty Harbor?" The kitten began sucking on his finger.

While my heart melted at Hitch giving the kitty some love, I managed to stay on point. I said, "He has other obligations. Even if he can help us, it won't be full time. We need this Kitty Castle set up like, right now."

The kittens tumbled over each other and Jasper. The truth was, they probably couldn't care less what their surroundings looked like, but I cared. Seeing all the dead plants, broken clay pots, and crushed plastic trays mixed with dirt, leaves, and discarded papers was no way to live.

Hitch stood up. "Let's get started then. There's nothing on my schedule. I might not be the best carpenter, but I can measure, cut and nail. Between the two of us, we can get it done. What do you think about that plan?"

I clapped my hands, startling two of the kittens. "That's a plan I can wrap my head around," I said, laughing at the strange trajectories of this day. I stood up next to Hitch, anxious to get started. "First, we need brooms and garbage cans to make this spotless before we start to build."

"I planned ahead for that, Sunshine." Hitch shot me his killer grin. "I went home for my truck and picked up supplies already. Do you want to sweep or pick up piles of trash?"

We headed outside to his pickup to get the brooms and pans. I remembered my garden.

"Before we get started, do you think we should move the bonsai tree?" I asked. Leaving it out in the open, especially after Conrad's visit, seemed like a disaster waiting to happen.

Hitch shook his head as he lowered the tailgate. "Tilly's keeping her eagle eye on your yard. She'll go out with guns blazing to scare away anyone who starts snooping around," He turned my face toward his, and I diverted my eyes away from his intense gaze. "Is something else going on you need to tell me?" he asked, his voice now soft with concern.

Great, my emotion-lined face gave me away again. With a deep inhale and slow exhale, I gave him the news. "Conrad was here before you arrived."

I thought his eyebrows would fly off his forehead when I dropped that bombshell.

"What did he want? I hope he didn't try to convince you that he only has Harry's best interest in mind. Because you can't trust *anyone* who'd break into their friend's apartment. Never, Sunny." His jaw clenched and his brown eyes turned to the color of coal in a stony glare. Hitch made zero effort to hide his feelings about Conrad.

"Does Harry have a wife?" I asked. Coming at this information from the back end might be easier.

Hitch shrugged. "He never mentioned having a wife. Why?"

"Here's the thing. Conrad said Harry needed money to pay for his wife's care. She's in a nursing home somewhere around here. He—"

"Was going to sell the bonsai tree?" Hitch asked. "That doesn't even make sense. Why hire me to protect it if he planned to sell it?"

"Not sell it, Hitch. Conrad was going to steal it but it was Harry's plan. Then he'd make an insurance claim. Was it insured?"

Hitch thought about that, then nodded. "Yeah. Harry hired me because insurance required that he have security." He laughed bitterly. "He needed me for security so he could scam the insurance company? I can't believe it. What a piece of garbage. I bet he shot me, so I didn't shoot Conrad."

"Conrad didn't think Harry's gun was part of the plan."

A sneer crept across Hitch's face, marring his rugged features. Can't say I blamed him, though, when he said, "I still don't believe that snake. What other whoppers did he tell you?"

Hitch gripped my arm a shade too tightly. I rubbed his hand, and he relaxed his hold. He was angry, and it was my fault. Well, not exactly my fault, except that I told him all this stuff that Conrad dumped on me. Isn't that what partners should share?

"Here's the real clincher," I said. "Conrad stole the bonsai tree from Maxine's house and put it in Gina's car. He wants me to find out if she still has it." I felt my lips twitch. "At least we have the upper hand on that part of Conrad's story."

Hitch's face fell. "And you told him that it's planted in your rock garden?" He held his head in his hands. Apparently, Hitch didn't see the irony the way I did or think I could keep a secret.

"No! Come on Hitch. Don't turn me into your enemy. I'm only telling you what Conrad told me. We have the tree and the only person who knows that is Gina. But she doesn't know what we did with it. Just in case she has a change of heart, I think we should move it somewhere else. I don't want it out there in my garden. Someone will see it."

"Yeah. Sorry for sniping at you. I just don't trust Conrad and what you just told me is really upsetting. Forgive me?" His eyes filled with a mixture of sorrow and anger and showed me a rare window into his emotions.

"Of course." And I meant it with all my heart.

Instantly, though, he was full of energy again. "You're right about the bonsai. We need to move it now. And then I want to find out *if* Harry's wife exists, where she is. Did Conrad tell you her name?"

I had to think about it for a couple of seconds. "Yes. Charlotte."

Cleanup forgotten, we jumped into Hitch's truck, with Jasper in the back seat, and made it to my house in record time.

"Do you see Tilly in her window?"

My heart sank. Tilly's head rested on the back of her chair and her mouth hung open. I could almost hear her snores. When I looked for the bonsai, all I saw was a flock of pink flamingoes scattered in my yard.

Our eagle eye guard fell asleep on the job leaving an opening for someone to steal the bonsai.

This was bad.

21

"*T*illy!" I yelled as I barged inside without knocking.

"In here, Sunny," she answered, wiping drool from the edge of her mouth and trying to sound like she hadn't just woken up.

I'd seen this act before.

"Where's the fire?" she asked like *I* was overreacting "I haven't seen anything happen on our street." She blinked several times, giving me her innocent look.

What could I say? At this point, I supposed it didn't matter.

She looked at me, then out the window. "Oh. Did I fall asleep for a minute?"

"Probably more than a minute." I sank onto her couch. "The bonsai tree is gone."

"And, my flamingoes?" I knew she was trying to lighten up my mood.

"All dead." I tried to grin but couldn't manage.

"I'm so sorry. The warm sun caressing my face and Pinky's loud rhythmic purring must have made my eyelids heavy." She stroked her big orange cat who was a constant fixture on Tilly's lap. "Any idea who stole it?"

Hitch stomped inside with Jasper at his heals. "Jasper was nosing around the area and found this." He held up a watch with a broken band. It was practical and plain, but the gold trim made it look expensive. "I think that whoever stole the bonsai tree, lost it in their rush."

He handed it to me, and I turned it over to find a heart engraved on the back. A gift? Someone would want it back I bet. I slipped it into my pocket.

"One of my flamingoes must have put up a valiant struggle," Tilly said. She shrugged when we both looked at her. "Maybe?"

The absurdity of her comment plus the image of a pink plastic flamingo yanking on someone's watch band finally made me laugh.

Hitch shook his head, but he laughed, too. "Yeah, that's probably exactly what happened," he said. "I'll go interview all of them to get the identity of the thief."

Tilly and I fell into uncontrolled giggles. It was

ridiculous, but sometimes laughing is absolutely the best medicine when a situation hits rock bottom. Or, in this case, bonsai bottom. I giggled again.

Tilly's expression turned serious. "Why did you come back? Did something happen to make you think the bonsai wasn't safe?"

"One of the flamingoes told us," I said, unable to end the silly flamingo conversation.

Hitch groaned. "Enough is enough. This really isn't a laughing matter."

"You're right, Hitch, but I have one important observation to add." Tilly leaned forward. I slid to the edge of the couch cushion wondering what was coming next.

Tilly narrowed her eyes at me, then at Hitch. With a deadpan expression, she said, "Those birds look innocent and artificial but... you never know what they're up to when no human is around watching."

I choked, then roared with laughter. I clutched my sides. "Please... stop. You're killing me."

"Well," Tilly stood up, "the only solution to that problem is—"

"Mint chocolate chip ice cream," I yelled, finishing Tilly's thought. Her one and only go to solution for just about every problem involved mint chocolate chip ice cream in one form or another—straight from the container, in a bowl with hot fudge sauce and whipped cream, an ice cream cake, or in a shake. Today I'd opt for hot fudge sauce and whipped cream.

"Come and help me, Sunny. Hitch is already lost on his phone and doesn't need to listen to our chatter." Tilly pulled me along to the kitchen.

She hauled the container of ice cream out of the freezer, and I grabbed the bowls from the cupboard.

"Tell me," she said. "Who do you think stole the bonsai tree?"

"Honestly? I don't know what to believe. Conrad stopped by and gave me an earful. It could have been Maxine checking in every place she could think of and got lucky when she drove by my house."

Tilly leaned against the counter and helped herself to a spoonful of ice cream from the container. "Let me get this straight. Someone stole the bonsai tree from Maxine's house, and you think she stole it from your yard? If it was hers to begin with, it's not stealing."

I arranged spoons and napkins on a tray and tilted my head at her. I thought we'd been over this. "It's technically not hers, Tilly. Unless she can prove she either bought the bonsai and orchid collection from Harry which is doubtful, or he *gave* the whole collection to her which is beyond believable, all the plants belong to Harry's estate."

"And who gets that?" Tilly scooped ice cream into bowls. "Hot fudge sauce, too?"

"What kind of question is that? I'll get it." I opened the fridge and found a new jar in the door. Thirty seconds in the microwave and we'd be in business. "Conrad told me he took the plant from Maxine's house and put it in Gina's car. He claims he wants to get it to the rightful owner, which *he* says is Harry's wife." I had my eye on the timer as my mouth was watering for that fudge sauce.

Tilly put the ice cream away and said, "That takes care of that, then. She'll come around to identify the body and claim the plants. That part of the mystery is solved."

I poured hot fudge sauce on the ice cream and Tilly topped each bowl with a squirt of whipped cream. I preferred to whip real cream myself, but she liked the sound the cream made when it shot out of the can. Tilly picked up her bowl and dug in as she left the kitchen.

I followed with the other two bowls on a tray. "No, Harry's wife won't be showing up. She's in a nursing home. According to Conrad, she's in an Alzheimer's unit somewhere here in the Blueberry Bay area."

"Oh. That must be the Best Care Nursing Home in Misty Harbor." Tilly said. "It's the best facility around."

I handed Hitch his bowl of ice cream. "Did you hear what Tilly said?"

"No. I've been searching for nursing homes."

I looked at Tilly and rolled my eyes. "See what I have to put up with?"

"What?" He took a giant spoonful of ice cream. Hot fudge sauce dripped down his chin, but he caught it with his finger before it splattered on his shirt.

"Charlotte might be at the Best Care Nursing Home," I said. "Tilly says it's the best place around, right next door in Misty Harbor."

"What are we waiting for?" he asked, setting his bowl on the coffee table. "Let's go and visit."

Tilly pointed to Hitch's bowl. "Finish that first. Then we'll leave."

I wasn't about to argue with that command.

"We? You're coming, too?" he asked, obviously not pleased with Tilly butting in. I couldn't blame him. Her unpredictable style always risked unintended consequences.

"Of course, I'm coming. It's a nursing home." Tilly's bottom lip trembled, and she dabbed at the corner of her eyes. "In fact, I'm driving. I need to visit my dear friend Charlotte to give her my condolences over the loss of her beloved husband, Harry." She added a loud sniff, sniff for emphasis.

I grinned. If anyone could pull off an act like

that, it was Tilly Morris, world traveler and amateur actress.

Hitch shook his head. He knew when the best action was a mouthful of ice cream to help him keep quiet.

We finished in silence, but Tilly smirked in between bites.

Would we find Charlotte at the Best Care Nursing Home, or was Conrad leading us on a wild goose chase?

22

*T*he drive to the Nursing Home was uneventful, unless I counted Tilly practicing her tearful heartbroken friend routine as she zipped along the scenic road to Misty Harbor.

It was hard to ignore...Tilly, not the stunning Blueberry Bay scenery.

"Oops!" Without warning, she slammed on the brakes and swerved her little green beetle into a parking spot on Misty Harbor's Main Street. Loud honking from behind and the flash of a swerving truck had me praying we wouldn't get side swiped, sending the side of the car crushing into me.

Once I knew I was still in one piece and managed to make my voice work, I screamed, "What are you doing?"

Tilly said calmly, "The flower shop is still open."

She turned off the engine and grabbed her fanny pack. "I want to buy a bouquet for Charlotte."

I rolled my eyes at Hitch. "We aren't even sure she's at this nursing home, Tilly. You'll look ridiculous walking in with flowers for a nonexistent patient."

"Don't be silly." She flicked her wrist dramatically. "It will look much more realistic. If Charlotte isn't there, I'll let the tears flow, and make up some kind of sad story about my own failing memory. Don't worry, Sunny. I know how to act like an old person when I have to."

She knew how to act like something, but I wasn't sure exactly how to describe it. I kept that comment to myself.

Tilly hopped out of the car and ran into the flower shop.

"She's really into this, isn't she?" Hitch said, turning around to face me. "I hope we're not making a mistake."

"Too late for that. She's playing the part for all it's worth. What if there is no Charlotte at the nursing home?"

"I've been thinking about that, too. I suppose she could be at a different facility."

"Or, Conrad spun a sad story for some reason."

"I still think he's after that bonsai tree for himself," Hitch said. "He'd know who's interested in buying it. I'm sure that's something he and Harry discussed before they concocted the crazy plan to scam the insurance company. Harry mentioned different names to me while I was working, but I never thought he'd sell."

"It's clever if he pulls it off," I said. "If he can convince everyone that he's taking the bonsai for Harry's wife —"

"That no one knows about," Hitch filled in. "He can do what he wants with it — keep it or sell it — who would know? If everything he said about Charlotte is true, she's in no condition to get what's rightfully hers."

Tilly opened the door, slid back onto the driver seat and passed the bouquet back to me. I stuck my nose into the middle of the flowers, inhaling deeply.

"Ahhh… aroma therapy at its best. This is beautiful, Tilly. You really went all out for someone you don't even know. Freesias, iris, delphinium, and what's this? Eucalyptus? Very nice." I noticed an envelope. "A card, too?"

"Of course. Go ahead and read it."

I slid the card out and read, *"To my dearest friend, Charlotte. Your loss is my loss. Harry is forever in my heart. Love, Mildred."* I choked. "Mildred? Who are you pretending to be?"

"If you must know, that's my legal name. I've never liked it, and I don't even know when my

father started calling me Tilly. I think it had something to do with me running around singing Silly
Tilly instead of Silly Milly which I guess I couldn't
say. Anyway, it made my father laugh and the nickname stuck. I was always Silly Tilly in my father's
eyes."

Hitch grunted and mumbled, "Silly Tilly and
nothing has changed."

She swatted his arm, but we all chuckled
because the name fit her to a T.

"I signed it Mildred, just in case someone sees
the card. No one will have a clue who Mildred is,
but there's a slight chance that someone could
recognize Tilly. I'm probably the only one for miles
around."

"Thank goodness for that."

"What did you just mumble, Sunny? Oh, it
doesn't matter. I'm sure it was a compliment to my
unique personality. Now you two know my secret.
It's how I go incognito in these undercover type
situations." She glanced at me in the rearview
mirror. "Don't you dare tell anyone or I'll have to
kill them."

"Oh, boy. Hitch, we've created a monster."

Tilly hit the gas, sending my head crashing
against the headrest, but I clutched the bouquet,
saving it from flying around in the car. Another
near-death experience of screeching tires and

honking horns was a reminder to never let Tilly drive me anywhere. Ever again. First, though, we had to survive this trip.

"That was fun, wasn't it?" I love to live dangerously." She turned her head and grinned.

Tilly slammed on the brakes, barely missing the stopped car in front of us. "Watch out!" Hitch yelled, ramming his hands onto the dashboard.

Tilly just tossed her head and laughed. "Another close call. Relax you two. I haven't been in an accident in ten years, and that one wasn't even my fault."

At least she kept her eyes on the road as we continued slowly through Misty Harbor, past the Little Dog Diner, the Blueberry Bay Grapevine, and Creative Designs across the street.

A few miles later, Tilly turned into the entrance of Best Care Nursing Home and parked in the patient drop off spot.

"Tilly, you can't park here," I said.

"Oh, stop being such a worry wart, Sunny. I'll drop off the flowers, say something sweet to Charlotte, and be back here in two shakes of a cat's tail."

"Don't you mean a lamb's tail?"

She paused her manic activity of stuffing keys in her bag, futzing with her hair, and pursed her mouth. "Doesn't matter. You knew what I meant." She reached for the bouquet.

"Give me the keys," I said, holding my hand out, or no flowers. "Hitch will move your car to a visitor spot."

She grumbled and mumbled something incoherent, but finally tossed the keys to Hitch. "Don't scratch it," she said as she handed them over.

I handed her the flowers and she climbed out of the car. I took a deep breath, hoping that we didn't have to go inside and rescue her from an awkward situation.

Hitch jogged around to the driver seat, and I moved to the passenger seat. With any luck, Tilly would let Hitch drive us home so we'd make it in one piece. He moved the Volkswagen to the far end of the parking lot where we could still see the entrance.

"I'll leave the car running for a quick get-away when she comes out," Hitch said. "Or, we could just leave her here to fend for herself."

"Are you trying to tell me I'm overreacting?"

"A little. It's a nursing home, Sunny. She's not planning a bank robbery or anything criminal like that. So what *if* she makes a fool of herself?"

Well that was cruel. But he had a good point. "You're right. I guess I'm a little jumpy from so many unexpected things falling in my lap lately." I let Hitch keep an eye on the entrance while I scanned the parking lot. Maybe I'd see Conrad coming to visit Charlotte if he really was as concerned as he said.

Hitch squeezed my hand. "Everything will turn out okay."

"Sure," I said with little conviction. For all we knew, the killer was plotting to destroy us before we unraveled this maze.

I leaned forward trying to get a better view of the car parked opposite us. "Is that Gina?"

Hitch shaded his eyes from the glare. "It looks like her car. What's she doing here?"

I opened the door. "That's exactly what I want to find out, and I wouldn't be surprised if she has the bonsai tree in her trunk." For some reason, I'd unleased my frustration on Gina, who for no fault of her own, was in the middle of this mystery.

Hitch grabbed my arm. "Wait. Let's see if she goes inside, then I can pop the trunk, and she won't know we're on to her. Can you see what she's doing?"

"I think she's reading something... and maybe talking on her phone." I looked at Hitch, confused and curious. "What now?"

Before we could decide what to do, Gina started her broken down car and pulled out of her parking spot in a cloud of dust.

"Follow her," I said to Hitch. I snapped my seat

belt in place and braced for a quick take-off. "She might lead us to the bonsai tree."

"I can't do that. This is Tilly's car, and we can't just leave her here."

"Oh yeah, right." I pointed to the hospital entrance. "There's Tilly. Quick. Pick her up, and maybe we can catch up to Gina."

Hitch put the car in gear and swung around to head to Tilly. "Gina's long gone by now, Sunny. The bonsai tree will surface along with some answers, I imagine."

Tilly, with an energetic bounce in her step, stopped at the end of the walkway, then scanned the parking lot. She waved when we pulled up in front of her.

"Get in the back, Sunny. Hitch can drive but the co-pilot seat has my name on it."

I could live with that. Literally. I hopped in the back.

"So? Did you find Charlotte?" I leaned forward between the front seats, not wanting to miss any detail about her visit.

"Nope. She was moved this morning."

"Moved? Because Harry died and payments stopped?" How cruel I thought.

"The woman at the desk didn't know the details or couldn't tell me, but she felt terrible that I'd made the trip for nothing. She claimed that she doesn't know where Charlotte is now. Is that odd?"

"Maybe it's about privacy. At least you got to keep the flowers."

"Here. You have them, Sunny. You know me, I can't keep a plant alive if my life depended on it."

"Thank you. No one has given me flowers in, well, hmmm, a long time." I inhaled the sweet aroma. A bouquet of fresh flowers was one of life's many pleasures.

I saw Hitch glance in the rearview mirror. "Is that a hint, Sunshine?"

"Take it however you'd like." He winked at me before he turned his attention back to the road. I couldn't help but smile a little before my thoughts returned to our immediate situation.

Harry's valuable bonsai tree was the key to unlocking his murder.

Which one of the people stalking the bonsai killed him?

*E*ven a pillow over my head couldn't silence the racket in the morning. Between Jasper's barking and someone's frantic pounding on my front door, I gave up trying to get an extra few winks.

I glanced at my bedside clock and moaned. Half past six. Was another half hour of sleep asking too much? Jasper's wet tongue on my face answered that question.

"Okay, okay. What's the emergency?" I asked her, sniffing the air. Nope, no fire. Glad I eliminated that potential catastrophe, but I smelled something. The aroma of freshly brewed coffee filled my nose.

What?

I leaped out of bed and dashed down the stairs.

Hitch, all bright eyed and ready for the day, stood in my kitchen in his snug jeans and a t-shirt that hugged his muscles. But *I* wasn't paying attention to his sculpted body.

"Did you sneak in through Jasper's doggie door?" I asked, leaning against the door frame with my arms crossed. I snorted, imagining him half-way in and half-way out like he'd found me.

"Didn't have to," he said, handing me a cup of steaming coffee with just enough cream to turn it a sweet caramel color. My heart flipped when I realized he'd remembered how I liked it.

"Jasper let me in." Hitch made a grand gesture for me to sit down at my own kitchen chair like I was *his* guest. A bag from A Donut A Day shop on the table tempted me.

"Actually, your door wasn't locked, Sunny. You really need to be more careful, especially—"

"Because anyone will just walk inside, Hitch? I don't think so. Not with Jasper on the inside sounding like she's ready to bite an intruder's head off. You know, I've managed a-okay while you were off in New York playing security guard and getting yourself shot. So, which one of us needs to be more careful?" I shot him a glare that I hoped let him know that I got him on that one.

His lips twitched at the edge. *Not*, the response I

was going for. I resented how he thought he could just swoop back into my life and take charge like he hadn't broken my heart once already.

"We're *business* partners," I spit at him as if that explained all my hurt feelings.

"And, business partners make kind gestures for each other. That's all this is." He swept his hand over the table. "Coffee and something from your favorite shop in town to get your day off to a good start." He leaned toward me. "What did you think I was proposing?"

"Oh." Maybe I had read more into his visit than necessary. "I thought I did lock my door," I added a bit defensively as I opened the bag expecting my favorite cinnamon covered donut holes. Instead, I found a toasted breakfast bagel with egg and melted cheese on a layer of cream cheese, topped with a sprinkle of chopped chives. That was a close second.

"I already ate mine," he said. "Dig in." He pulled a giant dog bone from his pocket for Jasper who'd been sitting politely while a pool of drool puddled on the floor in front of her.

At least *I* hadn't drooled on the table.

Hitch leaned back and stretched out his long legs, bumping into my foot. "Here's what I'm thinking, Sunshine. Since it's still bright and early, we'll get our list of supplies put together to get started on the Kitty Castle, then drop in on Gina."

"Why Gina?" I said around a mouthful of bagel, spraying more than a few crumbs on the table. "Sorry." I covered my mouth.

Hitch grinned. "I'm glad that you're just being yourself around me, messy hair, pj's, and talking with your mouth full. Kind of like we're brother and sister, don't you think?"

"No! That's not at all what I'm thinking. You barged in without an invitation, and I had to see what was going on. If I'd known you were planning to visit—"

"You would have showered and put on clothes?" He hitched his eyebrows up in question marks.

"I would have double-checked that the door was locked," I shot back.

Hitch let out a deep belly laugh. "Well, I'm glad that's cleared up." He tapped his lip. "You have a big blob of cream cheese right there, Sunshine."

I finished the bagel in a pouty silence.

"Hey... truce? I'm sorry I barged in and woke you up. It's just that this missing bonsai tree is really bothering me."

I sipped my coffee. Perfection.

"Harry hired me to protect it, and I don't like to leave a job unfinished even though it's not really my job anymore. I don't know why, but I still feel responsible."

"Responsible or needing to find answers?" I

asked. "I mean, Maxine's involved. How did she get Harry's collection of orchids and the bonsai tree to begin with? And, Conrad's story seems logical, but who knows, especially with Charlotte going missing all of a sudden. Is he really looking out for her interest or his own? It's awfully convenient for Conrad that Harry isn't around to weigh in on his version of the whole break-in mess. Was it really Harry's idea to steal the bonsai tree and make an insurance claim?"

Hitch looked at me without commenting.

"I don't know, Hitch, this is a big tangled mess." I took another big bite. I could easily get used to this kind of surprise every morning.

Hitch crumpled up the bagel bag and threw it in my recycling bin, then sat down again. "I couldn't agree more, and you summed it up well. That's why I want to go to Gina's house. Just a friendly drop-in to find out what she knows about the bonsai tree."

"To catch her off-guard, you mean?"

He chuckled. "That's usually the best way to get information. If she came back and took the tree from your yard, I don't want to give her a chance to ditch it if she knows we're coming. But I'm not convinced that she *does* have it."

"I agree. What would be the point? If she was after money, how would she find a buyer? That leaves Maxine and Conrad."

"Or our friendly Officer Mick Walker. Don't forget that he was poking around."

I almost spit out the last bit of coffee I'd just gulped. "I'm not a fan of Mick, but I'm not sure he'd cross the line into stealing something, valuable or not."

"No, but I don't think he'd hesitate to help Maxine if he thought there'd be a nice payoff waiting. Maybe she said she owned it, and he believed her."

"Great. We have to watch our backs around that guy. I thought with the state police involved, we could forget about Mick."

Hitch drummed his fingers on the table, mulling over our puzzle. "Look at it this way, Sunshine. If Mick is involved with something illegal or unethical, he might have to resign."

I felt my lips spread into a big grin. "What are we waiting for?"

"For you to get dressed?"

I looked down at my cartoon jammies and felt my cheeks heat up. While sitting here with Hitch, eating and bickering like... well, brother and sister, I grudgingly admitted to myself that I'd completely forgotten I'd jumped out of bed and rushed downstairs half-dressed.

"Feed the kittens while I make myself presentable?" I said.

"I never said you weren't presentable, Sunshine." And there it was again, that mischievous grin that melted my heart.

I was in deep trouble.

24

I managed to shower and get dressed in ten minutes flat. Sure, I didn't take any time for make-up—over rated in my opinion—or a fancy hairdo—a quick twist of my wet hair in a ponytail worked just fine—before I took the stairs down two at a time. At the bottom, Tilly's voice came from the kitchen.

"What's the plan for today, Hitch?"

Please, please, please, figure out a way to keep her from coming with us. I sent the strongest silent plea to Hitch that I could manage. I loved Tilly with all my heart, but sometimes her enthusiasm caused a layer of problems I didn't need.

"We're planning a surprise drop-in on Gina," he said. I heard liquid pouring.

I walked into the kitchen and gave Tilly my

usual gushy greeting, then turned to Hitch. "Don't we have to pick up supplies for the Kitty Castle, Hitch? We want to get there before the crowds." I stood behind Tilly, gesturing with raised eyebrows, making cutting motions with my hands, and shaking my head. Please, Hitch, don't let her tag along.

"That sounds like fun," she said and accepted the mug of coffee he had just offered her. "You can snoop around Gina's yard while Sunny and I distract her. Should we bring along some donuts or something?"

My shoulders sagged. I was no match against these two when they got started on a mission. I'd have to make the best of it. "Yes, we'll bring donuts and Jasper. She'll be a good excuse for that walk around outside."

Tilly put her half-finished mug on my counter. "I'd best go get changed. Can't be seen in my jogging outfit if we're going visiting."

With Tilly out of earshot, I unleased my frustration. "Why are we taking her? You know she's a loose cannon at best. Do we want Gina to clam up and kick us out when Tilly asks some personal question like... oh, I don't know... where'd you hide the bonsai tree? We need a little subtley on this operation."

Hitch waved away my concerns. "I admit that Tilly can be in your face, but sometimes her pointed questions get good results. Besides," Hitch said, "she doesn't take no for an answer. You know that better than I do. If she's determined to come with us, she'll come regardless. Here's what we'll do."

I sighed knowing Hitch was right. Again. I loved Tilly, but sometimes she drove me crazy.

Hitch folded his arms on the table and explained his plan. "You go to Gina's door, and I'll wait in the car with Tilly and Jasper. Tell her you're just checking on her after what happened yesterday. You're making sure she's okay and hope nothing else has happened. How does that sound?"

"Fine, except Tilly won't stay in the car."

"We'll play that by ear. I might have to lock her in." He grinned. "Are you ready?"

"I guess so." I glanced at the kittens eating, pleased that Hitch had fed them. "See you two later," I said wishing I had more time to spend with them. Once we had the Kitty Castle finished, maybe they'd prefer to live there.

Hitch, Jasper, and I waited next to his truck for Tilly. It wasn't long before she arrived, decked out in a mid-calf length tie-dyed skirt and white gauzy blouse. She had a bright pink scarf tied around her gray hair. The transformation was... well, a Tilly-like imposter.

She twirled around with her arms out to the side, sending her skirt twisting around her legs.

"What do you think? Friendly but not too formal? I don't want to scare that poor girl after what she's been through. I call this my grandma's-come-for-a-visit look."

I whispered to Hitch. "She's never going to agree to wait with you in the truck after she put her visiting skirt on."

"Looks perfect, Tilly." Hitch opened the door of his truck and offered his hand. "Hop in."

"I have to sit in the back?"

"With Jasper," he said making it sound like the best seat in the vehicle. "You can have the front on the way back."

"No thanks. I'll take my own car and follow you. Here." She handed me a walkie talkie. "So, we can coordinate our strategy."

I should have known she'd add another dimension to our plan, but I took it without arguing.

We finally managed to leave while the queen followed us, dictating specific instructions for the type of donuts I should get.

Her voice came through the walkie talkie over some background hissing. "Nothing too unusual. Maybe a couple honey-glazed, a couple chocolate-glazed, and maybe a couple powdered. That way, there's something for everyone."

I scowled at Hitch, not that any of this was his

fault, and picked up my walkie talkie. "Those are all *your* favorites, Tilly."

"Well, no one likes cinnamon except you, so I guess you could get *one* of those."

Hitch tried his hardest not to laugh. Without much luck. "Maybe Gina doesn't even like donuts. What then?" he asked.

"I heard that, Hitch. We'll eat them all," Tilly said without missing a beat. And, I didn't doubt that she would.

Donuts were the least of our problems at this point. Finding answers topped my list. After a quick stop for the donuts, Hitch drove to Gina's house. She lived on a quiet, tree-lined street outside of town.

Her driveway was empty when we pulled up.

"Well, what do we do now?" Tilly asked, pulling to a stop behind Hitch's truck and still talking through the walkie talkie.

"Wait in your car," I said. "I'll knock just in case she's here."

I walked to the front door, glancing in the front windows for any sign of activity. Just as I was about to knock, Tilly pushed me out of the way and did the honors.

"I didn't get all dressed up to sit in my car, Sunny."

I glanced at Hitch who shrugged his shoulders as if to say, well, I tried.

The door opened.

"Hello?" a tiny voice greeted us.

"Good morning," Tilly said in her best cheerful tone, but I could tell she was caught a little by surprise, too. "Is Gina home?"

"Are you Gina's friend? Please come in. I was getting a little lonely here all by myself."

I hated leaving Hitch in the truck wondering what was going on, but I couldn't very well wave him in now. This poor woman might think it was some kind of home invasion.

We went inside and she closed the door.

"I'm Mildred and this is Sunny," Tilly said. Great, she used her incognito name but outed me.

"I'm Charlotte," our hostess said.

Harry's wife? I almost fell over.

When I looked at Tilly, her eyes bugged wide open. I'm positive the tiniest of a breeze would have toppled her.

What was going on?

25

*C*harlotte led us into a comfy living room. "Would you like tea?" she asked, giving us a friendly smile.

"Oh," I handed her the bag from A Donut A Day shop. "We brought this, but if Gina's not here... " I left my thought unfinished hoping Charlotte would insist that we stay anyway.

She did. "Don't be silly. Sit down, and I'll make the tea."

Tilly, having recovered from her initial shock, said, "We'll help you." She took Charlotte's elbow, chatting as if they were long lost friends as we headed to the kitchen.

This would be interesting. Tilly, who could barely boil water helping in someone else's kitchen.

"Where's that young girl who lives here?" she asked as I tagged along letting Tilly take charge.

Charlotte turned toward Tilly with her brow wrinkled in confusion. "I'm not sure, dear."

Charlotte stopped as if she couldn't walk and think at the same time. "She left a little while ago in a big rush and said she'd be right back." She laughed. "My memory isn't what it used to be. To be honest, after living in that other place, I don't like to be alone anymore so I'm glad you're here."

Now, I felt like a heel. This kind woman was just lonely for company, and we were digging for information.

"Have you lived here with Gina for long?" Tilly asked.

"Oh, no. I'm a little confused about everything, but for some reason I couldn't stay in that other place anymore. I liked it there. We had games and painting, but that young girl said I had to go with her."

Charlotte put the tea kettle on the stove but forgot to turn on the burner. Maybe she had a bit of dementia after all, but nothing like Conrad had led me to believe.

Her hair was nicely combed, and she wore a stylish dress with a cardigan sweater buttoned all the way to her neck, and she had on sensible shoes. Glasses hung from a chain around her neck. She was, at least from my first impression, a friendly grandmother, happy for a bit of company.

"You sit down, and I'll fix the tea," Tilly said, gently leading Charlotte to one of the kitchen chairs. She turned on the burner and asked, "Which cupboard has the cups?"

"I'm not sure, dear. Just hunt around. I don't mind."

"Is Gina at work?" I asked.

"Gina? I don't think that's where she said she was going." Charlotte looked off into space like she was trying to recall something important, like who the heck was Gina.

Tilly handed me a plate for the donuts as she bumbled her way from cupboard to cupboard finding cups, tea, spoons, and sugar. I was impressed. She managed better in this stranger's kitchen than she did in her own. Maybe it was the role-playing that she was so good at.

Just as the kettle whistled, the front door opened.

My heart jumped into my throat. How would we talk our way out of this awkward situation?

"Grandma? Are you making tea? I told you not to turn the stove on while I was gone." Gina walked into the kitchen and stopped dead in her tracks. "What's going on?" she said when she saw us.

Her face told me nothing except for registering shock.

"We have company, dear," Charlotte said beaming with delight. "They brought donuts."

Tilly hugged Gina and kissed her on both cheeks. "It's so good to see you and your Charlotte is adorable. We didn't know she's your grandmother. Would you like some tea, too?"

"Okay." Gina looked at me, but it felt more like she'd like to shoot me than share a cup of tea with us. "We'll be right back." She pulled on my arm. "I want to show you something outside."

This was getting weirder and weirder but I followed her. What choice did I have?

"We'll save the cinnamon donut for you, Sunny. Which one do you want, Charlotte?" Tilly asked before Gina slammed the door closed behind us.

"What are you doing here?" she hissed at me. "You have no right to barge in on my grandmother."

"We came to see you, and she invited us in. She's lonely," I said. It was the truth even if it was a lame excuse.

"Your grandmother was Harry's wife?" I blurted out.

"*Was* is right. That horrible man had her locked up in that nursing home and wouldn't even let me visit."

Tears streamed down Gina's cheek.

"He taunted me and had me banned from the premises. Until he was dead. Then he couldn't stop me because *I'm* her next of kin."

I stroked her arm. "Why would he do that?"

Gina sniffled and wiped away the tears with the sleeve of her shirt. "He convinced everyone that he was a wonderful, caring husband and only wanted the best for her. But, you know what he did?"

I shook my head.

"He tried to steal her blind. All the money for that posh apartment in New York? That was hers. He sold all her heirlooms. She told me that a while ago. All that was left was her bonsai tree and orchid collection."

I couldn't believe what I was hearing. What a twisted mess. Poor Gina. Poor Charlotte.

"Did *you* kill Harry?" I blurted out without thinking. Who in their right mind would admit to murder?

"Believe me, I would have if I'd had the opportunity." She sagged against her front door. "I haven't dared to say this out loud... but I'm glad someone killed that man." Her eyes begged for compassion, or something. "I need your help."

I couldn't say no.

Hitch opened the door of the truck and Jasper bounded up to us, wagging her tail.

"Gina!" Hitch said. I didn't hear much compassion in that one word. "I found Harry's bonsai tree in the trunk of your car. It doesn't belong to you."

"You're right." She stood tall and stared at Hitch and held up her phone. "I could have you arrested for trespassing," she threatened.

She had a good point, but I didn't think either one of them would be heading to the police any time soon. This was a show down if I'd ever seen one.

Gina sighed and looked away. "It belongs to Charlotte, my grandmother. She's inside."

Hitch, normally cool, calm, and collected, blinked, then blinked again. "Harry's wife is your grandmother?"

"Yes. And I'm trying to save what's left of her possessions from that thief that you worked for."

I could tell something was going through Hitch's mind from the way he chewed on his bottom lip. Probably the same things I was trying to sort out for myself. If Harry and Conrad had been in cahoots to fake the theft of the bonsai tree in order to scam the insurance company, they were really stealing from Harry's wife.

If Gina's story was true.

The big question still remained: who killed Harry?

26

"*L*et's go inside," Hitch said, taking Gina firmly by the elbow.

That sounded like a good idea to me. "But what about the bonsai tree?" I asked. "If you broke into Gina's trunk so easily, someone else might, too."

"Conrad." Gina said, her voice filled with accusation. "All I heard while I was working at Maxine's house was 'Let's do this or let's do that with the bonsai tree.' They couldn't agree about anything. That's why I think Conrad took it and put it in my car. That way, he could convince Maxine to just sell the tree when he stole it back from me."

Hitch scanned up and down the street. "Have you seen him around here?"

"I haven't noticed, but I've been busy moving

Grandma and getting her settled in here. If he did come around, I didn't see him."

"It's only a matter of time, Hitch. Maybe you should stay out here with Jasper, just in case he does come around and that way, Jasper won't scare Charlotte." I added. My big gentle giant could be intimidating.

"Oh, that's okay. Bring Jasper in. Grandma loves dogs and it will be good therapy for her." Gina opened the door. Jasper must have sensed she was needed inside. She wormed her way through the door and made a beeline to the voices in the kitchen.

"Gina," Hitch said, "you need to make a decision about the bonsai tree. You should just come clean with the police and explain the whole history before you get arrested for stealing it. Turn the table on Maxine and Conrad and put them in the hot seat. Can you prove it belongs to Charlotte?"

I guessed Gina didn't handle stress very well from the harried look on her face and the hesitation in her voice. "I don't know," she said. "It's probably grandma's word against theirs, and who's going to believe an old lady with a failing memory? I told Sunny I need help. I know I can't keep it safe from Maxine or Conrad or someone else who might discover its value. That's why I left it with you yesterday. But I took it back once I decided to sell it. I want grandma to have enough money to live comfortably for the rest of her life."

"Does she know your plan?"

She shook her head, her drab hair swinging around her shoulders like a veil. "I'm not sure she'll understand what's going on. I had a lot of trouble convincing her to move out yesterday. She said she didn't want to leave, but I had no choice. Harry hadn't paid her bills for the past month, and I don't have the money to keep her there. Selling the bonsai tree will give her options I can't provide."

This was a tough situation for Gina. She wanted to do the right thing, but was it right to take that choice away from Charlotte?

"Listen," Hitch put his hand on her shoulder. I had a flash of how comforting that gesture could be. "Try not to worry. First, you need to find a safe hiding place for the plant. It only takes two quick twists to pop your trunk open. Besides, driving around with it in your trunk is only asking for broken branches and then the value plummets."

Gina's eyes filled with worry. "I hadn't even thought about that. I'll bring it inside and put it upstairs. Grandma can't do the stairs, so I won't have to worry about her seeing it and getting upset."

Hitch walked toward Gina's car. "I'll get it. You can keep your grandmother occupied while I take it upstairs. Later, we can discuss possible names of people who might want to buy it. While I was working for Harry, I heard him talk about some people who'd love to own it."

"What about Maxine?" Gina asked. "I know she wants it. I was all set to ask her before Conrad ruined everything by stealing it and putting it in my car." She dropped her head into her hands in despair. "I think he killed Harry, and I'm afraid he'll try to kill me next."

I wondered if Gina was right. Conrad was involved in every step of that bonsai tree's movements. What was he up to?

I pulled her inside the house. "Hurry up," I said to Hitch, and he showed off his speed and agility, getting the tree into the house and up to the top floor in a flash. The last thing we needed right now was for Conrad to drive up the street and see Hitch with the stolen bonsai. Or, worse than that, Officer Walker. Gina didn't seem capable of talking her way out of a paper bag at the moment.

I shuddered to think of the consequences for Hitch if he got caught right now. Having the tree would be a double whammy against him in the eyes of the law—revenge for being shot and possession of a valuable item. Some people killed for far less than that.

Fortunately, I was distracted from those

thoughts when Tilly yelled, "I need some help in here!"

What now? Gina and I raced into the kitchen to find Charlotte half off the chair, limp in Tilly's arms.

I quickly supported her dead weight to free Tilly's arms. She took Charlotte's pulse. "Slow and weak."

For Gina's sake she said, "I was a nurse in one of my previous lives." Tilly liked to refer to the variety of adventures she'd lived through as previous lives. I guess she thought it sounded theatrical.

Charlotte's eyes fluttered, all color drained from her face except for the slash of pink lipstick. She looked at all of us hovering around her. "What happened? I remember feeling a bit dizzy and then everything went black."

"You fainted, dear," Tilly explained. She turned her sometimes harsh voice to a tone of kindness and patience. "Has that happened before?"

"Yes. Did I eat anything yet?"

I glanced at the untouched glazed donut on the table in front of her. Tilly's chatter had probably distracted her from eating.

Gina crouched next to Charlotte, taking her grandmother's hands in hers. "I'm so sorry grandma. I shouldn't have left you alone, but I didn't know the line would be so long when I went to get you some orange juice." She smacked the side of her head.

"And, I left it in my car. I'll go get it. That will make you perk right up."

Tilly hovered, fanning Charlotte's face with her hand. "She's right, Charlotte. Some juice will take care of that dizziness. Do you think you can sit up now?"

"I'll try."

Tilly and I managed to straighten Charlotte on her chair. Jasper rested her head on Charlotte's lap and as she revived, she rewarded my sweet Newfie with gentle strokes on her head.

When Hitch walked in, he took one look at us supporting Charlotte and assessed the situation. "Sunny, a minute?"

I followed him into the other room. "You know she can't stay here alone. Is Gina going to be able to stay with her all the time?"

I shrugged. How would I know? "I think she's making it up as she goes. She's doing her best, but I doubt she had a clue what it meant to bring Charlotte home with her." I felt a stone drop in my stomach. "I guess we'll have to help."

Hitch gave me a grim smile. "Exactly. Charlotte should go home with Tilly. She has the nursing background and can stay with her until this mess is resolved. Do you think she'll agree to do that?"

"Tilly or Charlotte?" I asked.

"Tilly. I suspect that Charlotte will do whatever

Gina tells her to do." He looked around. "Where is she anyway?"

"She went to her car to get orange juice."

He walked right up to the front window. "I don't see her." In a couple strides, Hitch was out the door, checking Gina's car, and then the street. He slammed a fist into the palm of his other hand.

I ran outside. "What happened?"

"I'm not sure, but Gina's gone. I heard a vehicle's tires squeal around the corner at the end of the street when I came outside, but I didn't see it."

"You think someone kidnapped her?"

"That makes about as much sense as anything else that's happened recently, Sunny. And, if that *is* what happened, it has to be Conrad. He's the only one who knows that Gina has the bonsai tree. Maybe he was in the process of looking in her car, then he panicked, and grabbed her instead when she came outside."

Was this tree worth one life and now, maybe another?

27

I slid my phone out of my pocket.

"What are you doing?" Hitch asked.

"Calling the police. This is out of control."

"You're right. I just wish they'd send someone besides Officer Walker. I can't stand that guy."

Hitch had a point, but I couldn't control who arrived after I dialed 9-1-1. I told the dispatcher my location and that Gina Pitman might have been kidnapped.

Sirens sounded almost as soon as I hit end on the emergency call. Of course, it was Officer Mick Walker who pulled to a stop in front of Gina's house.

Hitch rolled his eyes at me, then walked inside. Leaving me to explain the situation to Mick was the smart decision.

Mick hauled himself out of his SUV and walked up to me with his usual arrogant stride. "I hope this is a real emergency, Sunny," he said, smirking as he looked from me to the house, "and not some game you and Hitchner are playing." His insulting tone suggested the worst about me.

"Do you consider kidnapping to be a real emergency, Mick? Because if not," I flicked my hands shooing him back to his car, "leave right now and send someone more responsible. Please."

The please was an afterthought, but he wasn't the only one who could play the snark game.

He pulled his lips across his teeth, as if he was biting his tongue on a comeback. "Kidnapping *is* a serious crime," he said. "Are you sure?"

I glanced at Gina's car. The bottle of orange juice, still on the passenger seat. "The bottom line, Mick. Gina went outside to get her orange juice. Car's here, orange juice is here. Gina's gone missing. Her grandmother is inside, and she needs constant care. Gina came out to get that bottle of orange juice for her grandmother who just had fainting spell and within minutes… no trace of her. Gone. Vanished into thin air. I don't know how else to explain it." Explaining the situation to Mick made the whole event more real. And scary.

"Did you see any suspicious person hanging around?"

"No."

"Any suspicious vehicle? Maybe, a van?"

"No."

"Maybe she decided to take a walk."

"Seriously?" Gina thought someone was trying to kill her, but I couldn't tell that to Mick without explaining why.

I couldn't help it, Mick's tone of voice made me snappish. "I doubt she'd feel like meandering around town just for the fun of it with her grandmother needing so much care," I said matching him scowl for scowl.

Okay, Mick had to ask those questions. But my patience, thin before he'd arrived, reached my limit.

Mick walked away, talking into his radio. I tuned him out. I could only hope they'd figure out how to find someone who'd disappeared without a trace. I walked around Gina's yard, thinking and kicking the dirt absent mindedly. Was there anyone besides Conrad who might want Gina out of the picture? Maxine? Or, was it possible that Gina just took off because this was all more than she could handle? She couldn't get far on foot, though. And, the bonsai tree.

I grabbed the orange juice from her car and went inside. All of this would be hard, no impossible, for Charlotte to understand. But that's who needed our attention first.

"Are you feeling a little better now, Charlotte?" I heard Tilly ask when I got inside. They sat next to each other on the couch with Jasper's head resting on Charlotte's lap.

"Yes. Is that girl still here?" She looked around. "Where is she?"

"She had an errand to run, but she asked me to bring in your orange juice. Would you like a glass?" I held up the bottle, got a puzzled look from Tilly, but a nod from Charlotte.

"That would be very nice, dear. Thank you."

I was happy to see that Jasper was enjoying the constant ear massage.

"Where's Hitch?" I asked Tilly wondering how he could disappear in this small house.

"He came inside without saying one word. I helped Charlotte to the bathroom, and then I heard the back door close. She stood up and pulled me away from Charlotte. "What's going on? Where *is* Gina? And, did I hear a siren pull up?"

Charlotte seemed content sitting with Jasper, so I nodded for Tilly to follow me to the kitchen. "Gina's missing," I said urgently as soon as we reached the other room. "I called 9-1-1, and Mick is outside calling for backup I guess. Hopefully, the police will be able to find her."

"Is this Mick's lucky day?" Tilly asked with more than a touch of sarcasm. "I'm not sure that guy can find his gun when it's in its holster strapped around his waist."

"Well, I had to do something. This is completely out of control. I wish I knew what Hitch is planning to do. I don't want him to get into trouble."

Then I had a sinking feeling in the pit of my stomach. "Did he go upstairs?" I asked Tilly.

I didn't wait for an answer. I shoved the orange juice into her hand and darted for the stairs. I tripped in my haste to get to the top but managed to keep from falling. One door was half open, so I looked inside I checked the only other room, just to be sure. A tiny piece of evergreen lay on the floor along with some scattered dirt, but the bonsai tree was gone.

Great. Hitch took the tree. Why would he do that?

I raced back downstairs. "Let's get Charlotte in Gina's car and drive her to your house. Quick," I said to Tilly. "If I can find the keys."

Tilly, for once acted instead of spending any time questioning me. "Shall we go for a ride, Charlotte? Gina will come later."

Well, that was probably a lie, but Charlotte's memory was such that she might not remember.

Tilly, stronger than her slight build suggested, looped her arm around Charlotte's waist and steadied her as they walked to the door. "You know, I have my special car outside. It's lime green and shaped like a bug. Want to ride in that today?"

"Oh. That sounds like fun, I love green."

Charlotte was a sweetie. I could see why Gina was so concerned about her and it made less sense that she'd walk away and leave her grandmother after just moving her into her house. I'd only just met her, and I wanted to do everything possible to help her. I stopped hunting for Gina's car keys.

Jasper walked out first. Mick was near the road talking with other police officers. Good, maybe they'd find Gina while Tilly and I took care of Charlotte. The only problem was that their vehicles had us blocked in.

"Get Charlotte in the car. I'll talk to Mick about moving out of the way," I told Tilly.

"No, you get her in. I'll talk to Mick," Tilly said. "I know exactly what will get them to move." She grinned her Tilly-loves-this-game grin and walked toward Mick.

"Mick, honey?" She raised her hand and waved to get his attention. I pretended I wasn't watching, but I managed to keep an eye on the activity while I helped Charlotte get in the car.

"We have to take Charlotte to her doctor. Could you move out of the way?"

Mick looked at Tilly, then at Charlotte and me. "Who's Charlotte?"

"Gina's grandma. She just moved in and, you know, she has a bit of a memory problem. With my nursing background, Gina asked me to keep an eye on her and, well," Tilly lowered her voice, but I could still just make out her words, "she's having some incontinence problems."

Mick held both hands up.

"You know," Tilly continued anyways, "wetting her pants? I think she might have a urinary infection. The sooner it's treated, the better."

Mick blushed and motioned for one of the other officers to get his car out of the driveway.

I couldn't help but snicker at his embarrassment from Tilly's information overload.

Mick looked at Hitch's truck and asked Tilly, "Is anyone inside the house?"

"Oh, I don't think so, but the front door's unlocked if you need to go check. Maybe there are clues to help you find Gina. Poor Charlotte keeps asking for her granddaughter."

Tilly tut-tutted and patted Mick's arm. "I know you'll do everything possible." She turned away from him but stopped.

I held my breath. She'd been perfect, and this was the time to just leave before she blew her act wide open.

She fluttered her eyelashes like a caricature of a ditzy blonde. "Did you find that missing banana tree yet?"

Oh, Tilly, you never cease to crack me up. I bent over to buckle Charlotte's seat belt and hide my laughter, watching the show out of the corner of my eye.

Mick's forehead wrinkled in confusion. "What banana tree? Oh… you mean the *bonsai* tree. Uh, no, not yet. Maxine is about to have a nervous breakdown over it as a matter of fact."

He leaned closer to Tilly and dropped his voice. "She told me what the plant is worth, and I almost fell over from the shock. It's still insured, she told me. So, if it doesn't turn up, and with Harry dead, someone gets that huge payoff."

"Who's the beneficiary?" I heard Tilly ask, ditching her senile old lady act, but Mick didn't seem to notice.

"Bene-who? Oh, I don't know." He laughed. "Knowing Maxine, she probably twisted Harry's arm to make *her* the beneficiary before —"

"She killed him?" Tilly said finishing that sentence without a blink of an eye.

He had to be the most oblivious person I knew. No, make that, oblivious, mean, and without a shred of empathy, which made for one rotten combination in my opinion.

I bet Maxine *was* about to have a nervous breakdown. I'd like to get a look at that insurance policy.

---

28

*T*illy got behind the wheel of her Volkswagen and slammed the door. It wasn't hard to tell she was royally ticked off. I thought she knew better by now than to let clueless Mick Walker get under her skin. Although, eventually he had that effect on everyone. Me, included.

"Did you hear what he said?" she asked me. If Tilly had the ability, daggers would be shooting from her eyes straight to Mick's heart.

"Yes, but let's get to your house," I said, hoping she wouldn't start ranting about the missing bonsai tree in front of Charlotte.

Jasper leaned through the two bucket seats and licked her cheek.

"Where did you say we're going?" Charlotte

asked, absently patting Jasper. I eased her back next to me where I was squished on the back seat.

"For a little drive." Tilly patted Charlotte's leg. Thankfully, she had returned to the present moment. I relaxed next to Jasper while Tilly chattered away to Charlotte.

"How'd you like to stop for lunch at my house? Does that sound like fun? I have a great big cat named, Pinky, and Sunny will make us something delicious to eat."

"I love cats," Charlotte said. "And tuna fish. Could we have tuna sandwiches?"

Tilly glanced at me in the rearview mirror with her eyebrows raised. I doubted she had any in her cupboard.

"Sure, I can handle that," I said. "Tuna fish sandwiches with a pickle and iced tea, a meal fit for three charming ladies."

Charlotte clapped her hands. "I love an adventure, girls. I can't wait."

And I loved guests who were easy to please.

Tilly swerved around the corner at the end of Gina's street, reminding me that I'd vowed never to ride with her again. I sighed. Nothing be done now except hope she stayed focused and didn't hit anything.

"Hey! There's Hitch." I tapped Tilly's shoulder.

"Pull over. I'll walk with him and meet you at your house."

I should have said to slow down, first. We ended up with the passenger side tires over the curb, but thankfully, we were in one piece. Tilly opened her door so Jasper and I could squeeze out. I wasn't sure if it was a mistake to leave Tilly alone with Charlotte, but I had to find out what Hitch was up to.

"I was hoping you might find me," he said, waiting for me to catch up to him and draping his arm around my shoulders in a comforting gesture. Jasper plodded along behind us, not bothering to even check any hidden scents. She was ready to be home, too.

"Where's the banana tree?" I asked.

"Huh?" He stopped and looked at me like maybe I'd transformed into a new person since he'd last seen me. "Banana tree? Are we playing eye spy or something?"

I told him about Tilly's conversation with Mick, which got a big snort from Hitch. "That's one of her better word slip-ups. And, to answer your question, it's hidden, but I don't want to leave it where it is for long. I didn't have many choices since I left on foot in a hurry. It's awkward to carry."

I had to speed up to match my steps with Hitch's long stride. "Why did you take it to begin with? Do you realize what kind of trouble you'd be in if Mick found you with that tree?"

Actually, I liked going out for a stroll with Jasper and Hitch. I just wished we weren't on the hunt for a killer. As Hitch kept reminding me. "Of course, I do, Sunny, but until I know if Gina is safe, that bonsai tree will remain in hiding. Don't worry, no one will find it."

"Mick told Tilly that the insurance policy is still in effect, and if the bonsai tree doesn't turn up, someone will get a big payment. He even suggested that Maxine twisted Harry's arm to make her the beneficiary. He thought it was funny."

Hitch started walking faster, the urgency of our mission propelling him on. "That's what Maxine said? I don't see how that's possible. The bonsai tree is a living plant. Why would anyone insure it without safeguards in place, forcing the owner to do everything possible to keep it secure?"

Did I have to be an insurance expert to figure this out? "Like hiring a round-the-clock security guard?"

"Exactly. And Harry kept records of the temperature and humidity that he sent daily to the insurance company. Plus, the policy cost a fortune to begin with. I never thought of this before, but maybe Harry shot me to make the whole break-in look more realistic. Except that Conrad bolted without the tree. Harry should have prepared him better." He picked up the pace again. I was getting a little out of breath, but he didn't notice. He said, "We've got to get to your house, get your car, and pick up the tree."

"And then what, Hitch? Turn it over to the police and say, yeah, well, we've known where it was ever since Gina dropped it off at Sunny's house but… but, what? Why didn't we just turn it in when we had the chance?"

I stared at him. I knew I was being ridiculous but this whole cat and mouse game was taking its toll on me. My nerves were shot.

"Because everything was pointing at me, Sunshine. It looked like I killed Harry for revenge and stole the bonsai tree for its value. We need the tree to flush out the killer."

Great. Did that make us thieves by association or just dumb?

When we turned onto my street, we spotted a cargo van parked in front of my house. A van? Didn't Mick suggest the kidnapper would be in a van?

"Hitch? Do you recognize that vehicle?" I asked. My voice shook. And Tilly brought Charlotte right into this potential trap. Had someone guessed our move?

"Let's just walk by like it's nothing and check in

the windows. If you're thinking that's the vehicle that was used to kidnap Gina, I doubt very much that they'd park right outside your house. Too obvious."

Maybe, but who could really predict what anyone would do. Like us, hiding the bonsai tree in a flock of flamingoes. It didn't work, though, so Hitch was probably right.

Hitch slowed down when we approached the back end of the van. The small back windows were covered, and it had no windows on the sides. What if they were watching us in the mirror and opened the door and pulled us inside when we got close enough?

Hitch stayed between me and the van.

Jasper woofed and ran, with her nose to the ground, right to her doggy door. I didn't like this.

"What do we do now Hitch? I think someone might be in my house."

"First, let's make sure Tilly and Charlotte are okay. We can keep an eye on this van and your house from her front window.

"What about Jasper? I think she went in through her doggie door. What if someone tries to hurt her?"

"You go to Tilly's, and I'll check out your house. I don't hear any barking so maybe someone dropped some food and made a trail to her door."

"Maybe." I jogged across the street and went into Tilly's house. Someone with a deep voice was talking. I'd heard that voice before.

"Sunny? Is that you? Come on in. Conrad has some interesting information."

Conrad. It was his van? Did he have Gina? Before I closed her front door, I got Hitch's attention and waved him to come over. If Conrad was up to no good, I wanted Hitch right there with us.

"Coming, Tilly."

"Did you make the sandwiches yet, dear?"

"Not yet. I'll just say hello then scoot back to my house." I walked into the living room. Conrad and Gina sat next to each other on the couch while Charlotte sat in Tilly's favorite rocking chair with Pinky in her lap.

It didn't look like anyone was tied up or held at gunpoint. As a matter of fact, it looked like a normal happy scene. But it made no sense.

What was going on?

29

*H*itch screeched to a halt at my side. We both stared at the group of people sitting in Tilly's living room who stared right back at us like we'd arrived with some important news.

Had we?

He looked at me with the same shocked expression I assumed was on my face. The silence buzzed in my ears as I tried to understand why Conrad and Gina were *both* sitting here together like long lost friends.

"Sunny, how about you and Gina go fix those sandwiches?" Tilly said, coming to the rescue and breaking through my stunned silence. "Hitch, you stay here."

Charlotte hummed and rocked and stroked

Pinky the whole time, an oblivious, satisfied smile on her face.

I nodded, not sure why Tilly thought I'd need help, but wasn't about to argue. Tilly had her reasons. She always did. "Come on Gina."

As soon as we were outside, I turned on her. "What's going on? You disappear, then show up here with *Conrad*? We thought he'd kidnapped you."

I unleased all my worry-fueled adrenaline that my system had converted to anger on her.

She took my arm. "Not here. Let's get in your house. Did Jasper track me to her doggie door?"

"She tracked something. Did you break into my house again?"

"I was looking for you, but when Tilly arrived with grandma, we went to her house.

Conrad and Gina were *we* now? I opened the door and let her enter first. Jasper lumbered over to greet us. First, with a friendly sniff for Gina and then she rewarded me with a tail wag before she lay down on her sun-soaked spot in the living room. Immediately, Stash and Princess Muffin attacked her. At least *this* seemed normal in the otherwise upside-down situation.

I crossed my arms and leaned against my kitchen counter. The sandwiches could wait as far as I was concerned.

Gina had other ideas. Without asking, she began

searching for the lunch ingredients. "Here we go. You think three cans of tuna fish will be enough?"

"Better use four. Hitch will want two sandwiches." What was I doing? I wanted answers, not food. I sighed but handed her a loaf of bread and pulled out the mayo and pickles from my fridge. "Okay. Explain everything while we get this done."

"It's not what you think, Sunny. At all."

I dug out a bowl from my cupboard and handed it to Gina while she opened the cans. "How do you know what I'm thinking?" I asked.

Geesh. Right now, I thought Gina and Conrad were acting like a couple of scallywags in cahoots involving a murder and theft. Not much annoyed me more than someone thinking they could read my mind. Well, Hitch got away with it because he was usually right but that was different. Gina didn't know me like he did.

Gina emptied the tuna into the bowl and mixed in the mayo while I lined up bread on the counter.

"Conrad didn't kidnap me," she said. "He gave me an ultimatum—get in or he'd call the police and say I stole the bonsai tree. I went with him willingly."

Now I understood Tilly's plan to separate Gina and Conrad. They couldn't coordinate their story beyond what they'd already planned together, brilliant on her part.

I fixed a pitcher of iced tea and found my wicker basket to pack our lunch.

"You see," Gina turned around so we faced each other. "I was in my car ready to drive off. When I saw grandma fall into Tilly's arms, I panicked. I realized I couldn't care for her properly and selling the bonsai tree seemed easy until I had to figure out how to actually do it. I didn't want to be responsible for damaging it and destroying its value."

She paused as she assembled the sandwiches. "And, the worst part? She doesn't really even know who I am." A tear slid down her cheek.

"But how could you trust Conrad? I said. I held up a finger to pause her explanation while I found the sandwich bags. I handed them to her and said, "You told me you thought he killed Harry and might kill you next. Why on earth did you agree to go with him?"

My brain swirled with questions and confusion.

She turned away and slapped pickles on the bread. I supposed I'd annoyed her with my questions, and she needed something to focus on.

"I was completely wrong about Conrad," she mumbled. "He told me he's been trying to protect the bonsai tree, first from Harry selling it, and now from Maxine just keeping it. The scariest thing he told me was that he thinks Harry was really trying to shoot *him*, not Hitch."

I gasped at what *that* implied. "Why does Conrad care so much about the bonsai tree?"

Gina looked at me again, gauging how much to tell me. Her eyes were about to flood over. "I never knew this until today." She looked up at the ceiling and blinked away her tears. "Harry was Conrad's father from his first marriage, before he married Charlotte."

"How could you *not* know that?"

"I never got to meet Harry's family," she said matter-of-factly. "You see, my mother hated Harry. She saw him for what he was—controlling and selfish. She tried to convince my grandmother to leave him. It didn't work. Grandma fell hard for Harry. She loved his flashy life style, I guess, even though it was mostly an illusion. After they married, Harry isolated her and got control over her life, forbidding her to have anything to do with my mother or me. Even years later, when he placed her in the nursing home."

Gina let out one sharp laugh like she was remembering an old sad joke.

"He made one mistake. As a way to inflict more hurt on me, he told me where she was, but he wouldn't let me visit. Harry held that kind of power."

"Over all those years, you never got to visit or

talk to your grandmother?" I asked, completely dumbfounded and enraged.

"Oh, Grandma managed to sneak me a letter on my birthday and Christmas, but no, I wasn't allowed to see her."

"And, Conrad? How'd he fit in all this?"

"Conrad spent a lot of time with them. Harry didn't shun his own flesh and blood. Charlotte knew Conrad better than me, her own granddaughter, but," she quickly added, "I blame Harry for turning her against me."

I had to let this marinate in my brain for a minute. "So, Conrad agreed to the insurance scam so Harry could get his money and keep the bonsai tree? Why?"

Gina nodded and wiped her eyes. "He says it was to help Charlotte. It was her tree and about all she had left. It's all such a waste."

"What is?" I asked.

"Everything." Her whole body shriveled from what I'd seen as an energetic if not completely together young woman.

"After we eat, will you take me back to my house?" she asked. "I need to be by myself for a while. Figure out my next step. I can't go back and work for Maxine after all this. There's really nothing for me here anymore."

"You're going to just walk away from Charlotte? Now that you can finally help her?"

She shrugged. "I don't know if she cares who she lives with. Conrad said he'd make sure she's taken care of."

"That's generous of him. I suppose that means he expects to keep the bonsai tree."

"I suppose."

"Okay." I said, because really, what else was there to say at this point? I stacked the sandwiches in my basket, tucked a bag of cookies in a corner, and added napkins in case Tilly was out. A likely possibility. Maybe Gina would have a change of heart over lunch. It wouldn't be the first time food forced a new perspective.

"What about Harry's killer?" I asked. Had everyone forgotten that brutality in the chaos surrounding the bonsai tree?

She flinched. "What difference does it make? The world is better off without him."

"But, do you think Conrad killed him?"

"I don't really care, Sunny. I have to think about myself."

Me too. I wanted a resolution to this murder to clear the taint from my property and new business.

I saw Hitch coming across the street just as Gina was leaving with the basket of food. Judging from the spring in her step, unloading all that information seemed to improve her spirits considerably.

"What's going on?" he whispered when he reached my front door. "You've been over here forever. Conrad's getting fidgety and Tilly's almost through her repertoire of whacky stories. No one wants to hear them again. Especially me."

Jasper, with Stash in pursuit, trotted over to Hitch. "No, you don't." I grabbed the escaping kitty and tucked her in my tote. I carefully juggled Stash without spilling a drop from the pitcher of iced tea. I dawdled long enough for Gina to disappear inside Tilly's house.

"Gina just unloaded a heap of information on me," I told Hitch. "Now we have to be patient to see where the chips land. I think some things are about to get sorted out. Big things." I added. "Did you learn anything from Conrad?"

"Like what? That he admitted he killed Harry or something important like that?" Hitch ran his fingers through his hair in his frustrated-out-of-patience gesture.

"The whole situation over there is like something straight out of a nightmare. Charlotte has been rocking and petting Pinky, sometimes smiling and sometimes mumbling something that makes no sense to me. I think she's a lot worse than she originally seemed. Conrad keeps tapping his foot and doing something on his phone while Tilly talks and talks. Tell me something you learned from Gina."

"Well, Harry was Conrad's father for starters. Bet you didn't see *that* coming."

"Really? Are you sure you can believe Gina?"

"Good point. Like I said, something is about to break. The truth has a nasty habit of revealing itself." I took Hitch by his arm and looked up into his green eyes, glad we were on the same team.

"Oh, one more thing." I said as I closed the door and we walked across the street. "Are you positive the bonsai tree is safe when you took it out of Gina's bedroom and hid it somewhere?"

"Yeah, it's safe.

I tapped my lips with my finger. "Good. Call Maxine and tell her to meet us at the greenhouse in a half hour.

"What makes you think she'll come?" Hitch asked. "I'm not exactly her favorite person lately."

"She'll come. Tell her you have some new information about the bonsai tree."

Hitch rolled his eyes. I hope you know what you're doing, Sunshine."

I just smiled and waited for Hitch to open Tilly's door for me.

Showtime!

30

*T*illy, *despite* her lack of hostess skills, had managed to find plates for everyone and serve the sandwiches. Miracles never ceased to amaze me. Maybe that wasn't fair. To be honest, Tilly always got the job done.

I carried in glasses and poured the iced tea.

"This is nice," I said after I sat down with my food. The situation was anything but nice, more like awkward or extremely uncomfortable. But hey, my goal was for everyone to relax so I made a little light conversation.

"It's not what I expected today, but still… nice," I said. "How about you, Conrad? How's your day going? Gina told me a little bit about your background."

I took a bite of my sandwich, suddenly,

ravenous. Also, having my mouth full helped keep me from spilling too much of my newly acquired information.

Gina and Conrad shared a look—hers, wide-eyed, and his, scowling. Good. Let them wonder what I might blurt out next. If she thought I fell for her pity party, she could think again.

"Grandma?" Gina said. "Don't forget to eat your sandwich. I made tuna fish just like you requested."

Charlotte squinted at Gina and scrunched her eyebrows. "Who are you? Do I know you, dear?"

Gina glanced at me, and I saw her lip twitch, sending me the not so subtle message: *Told ya so.*

"Charlotte?" I waited for her to look at me. "You've found a wonderful friend there in Pinky. I can tell you love animals."

Her smile radiated happiness. "I do, dear."

"Look what I brought over from my house?" I held up the wiggling kitten, too adorable for words. "This is Stash. I found four more kittens and the mama cat. Would you like to visit them after we finish eating?"

Charlotte held out her arms. "She looks so soft. Could I cuddle with her?"

"Of course." I carried her to Charlotte. Pinky, unhappy about sharing, hissed and jumped off Charlotte's lap. She sat on the floor and licked her paw before rubbing her ear pretending she couldn't care less about the little intruder.

"Oh dear. Did I upset the orange monster?"

"Pinky has a bit of an attitude, but don't worry about it, Charlotte." Tilly patted her lap and Pinky slowly walked over, jumped up, and circled several times before she curled up there instead. "I can't say I blame her. Sometimes, all this young, unbridled energy is just too much for me, too."

Who was Tilly trying to fool? She thrived on energy and excitement.

Charlotte held the kitten between her neck and shoulder. Stash's purring filled Tilly's room. "You have more? Can I see them, too?"

"Of course," I said. "I'll just clean up these dirty dishes. It'll only take a sec." I carried everything to Tilly's sink. When I turned around, I practically knocked Gina over.

"What are you doing?" Gina stood eye level with me, with her arms crossed. "She'll want to keep one of those kittens, you know. Harry never let her have a pet. He said her plants were enough bother." Her eyes blazed angrily.

I gave the dishes a quick rinse and loaded them in the dishwasher. "It's not your problem now, is it Gina? You're leaving."

"Yeah, well, that's what I told Conrad so he'd get off my back."

Ah, and the truth came out. I forced myself not to smile at this little admission. "What's Conrad's plan then if he thinks you'll be out of the way?"

She shook her head. "I wish I knew. I can't figure it out, Sunny. He took the bonsai tree from Maxine's house and put it in my car. Why'd he do that? I thought he was going to call the police, so I dumped it with you."

I wiped the counter, hoping she'd keep up this chatter and reveal something important.

"And then I forced the nursing home to let me take Charlotte to my house. They weren't happy, but I told them I'd be managing her finances so what choice did they have? I think they were glad to get rid of her when I said I'd sort out her bills as soon as possible. In order to do that, I needed to get the bonsai tree back from you. Dumb hiding spot, by the way. No one was fooled by that flock of pink birds in your rock garden."

"Really? I thought it was very clever." Where was she going with this?

"Driving around with it in the trunk of my car was a recipe for disaster with Conrad stalking my every move. I'm really glad Hitch put it in my bedroom, otherwise Conrad would have it now, and he'd probably be long gone. The only reason he's sticking around is to get the tree back from me. What am I going to do?"

I crossed my arms. "Gina," I said feeling a bit frustrated. "You just spent ten minutes bashing Conrad after you told me he'll take care of Charlotte. You dragged Charlotte out of the nursing home, and now you say she's too much for you to deal with. You can't have it both ways. You expect me to tell you what to do? Well, I don't have the answer."

I'd like to tell her to grow up and take responsibility for her actions instead of whining and playing the victim for all of her twenty-something years.

She didn't say a word.

"I'm taking Charlotte to see the kittens. You should come, too. A little more time spent with your grandmother before you leave town? Do you think Conrad will come?"

She let out a bitter laugh. "He won't let me out of his sight until he has that tree back. I don't think he plans to help Charlotte at all. All that talk about saving it for her? He's just throwing shade to cover his own intentions."

I couldn't agree more, but I didn't tell Gina what I was thinking because I suspected she was throwing a fair amount of her own shade around.

I wasn't quite ready to leave. "You know, Gina, Charlotte didn't eat much of her sandwich. I'd hate for her to have another fainting spell."

"I know. She fed more to the kitten than she ate."

I'd noticed that too. "I bet she has a sweet tooth. I tucked some cookies in the basket. How about you pass them around and see if we can get her to eat one or two."

"Can't you just give me a ride home first? I've had about enough of all this. You could tell everyone you need my help with something, and we'll be right back, that way Conrad won't know where I am. The more I think about him, the more he makes me nervous."

She sagged against the counter with a big dramatic huff.

"I suppose that might work." I pretended to give her suggestion lots of serious contemplation. "The problem is, what if he decides to leave, too? Where do you think he'll rush off to?"

"Hmm. I hadn't thought about that. He'd probably go straight to my house to find the tree."

"Exactly. It's much better if we all stick together to keep an eye on him. I don't think he'll go anywhere as long as you're here. You'll be safe as long as you stay with me. Right?"

"Unfortunately," she said. I didn't miss the sarcastic undertone.

It was a lot harder to get everyone in one place than I'd expected, but we were almost there.

I shooed her out of the kitchen. "Get the cookies, Gina. And see if you can get Conrad talking about the bonsai tree. You know, I heard that it's still insured. Do you know anything about that?"

"Who told you that? Who's the beneficiary?" Gina demanded, suddenly alert.

My goodness, I'd hit a nerve with my comment. A big one.

I drummed my fingers on the counter. "I think it was Officer Mick Walker who told me. I wonder where *he* got the information."

"Maxine, I bet. I saw firsthand how she had Harry twisted around her little finger. I'll bet she convinced him to make her the beneficiary if anything happened to him." Gina's eyes widened. "She killed him, got Conrad to steal the tree, and then plant it in my car to frame me. Don't you see it, Sunny? They're in on it together, Conrad and Maxine. Now, if Conrad gets the bonsai tree back from me, he can sell it, Maxine gets the insurance money, and I go straight to jail for theft and murder."

"How do you know Maxine had Harry twisted around her finger?"

"I was working when he showed up with his plants. He was all like, *please Maxine keep my plants here* and *I'll make it worth your while*."

"Did he talk to you? He must have recognized you as Charlotte's granddaughter."

"I was careful to stay out of sight."

"You didn't want to give him a piece of your mind about yanking Charlotte out of your life?"

It would seem like the perfect opportunity to confront him. And, dropped right in her lap, no less.

"And get fired? I needed that job, Sunny. It didn't matter though with Conrad scheming against me. He had Maxine's ear just as much as Harry did."

Gina described an interesting theory about Maxine and Conrad.

If I was her, I'd be worried, too.

31

I put the last of the lunch ingredients away with a deep sigh, more than ready to get to the greenhouse and check on my kitty family. Yes, my responsibility, and I was thrilled to have a plan to help them.

"Hey," Hitch said and held a half-eaten cookie toward me. "I managed to save this for you, Sunshine."

"Where'd the other half go?" I tried to look upset but laughed instead. It was no secret that these chocolate chip oatmeal cookies were Hitch's favorite. Although, it was also true that he'd never seen a cookie he didn't like.

I popped the cookie in my mouth before he changed his mind and snatched it back.

He gave me a sheepish expression. "Sorry.

Conrad helped himself to the last tuna sandwich, and I was still hungry. You know, he's not so bad now that I've stopped blaming him for my injury. He didn't pull the trigger... doesn't even own a gun."

"You might even have more sympathy for him when I tell you what Gina said."

"Oh?"

"She told me that Conrad thinks Harry was trying to shoot *him*, not you. What do you think about that? Gina's been throwing all kinds of theories around, so it's hard to know what's true, what she's made up, or a combo of both."

"I never considered that angle. Why would Harry shoot *him*, though? What would be the motive?"

"To make the whole break-in more realistic? Just like you said, but you got hit and not Harry."

"I suppose it's possible, but we'll never know, will we? Harry's dead, and I don't think we're any closer to knowing who the killer is."

I smirked. "I think we are. Just wait until Gina and Conrad and Maxine are all together at the scene of the crime. I'll bet there will be plenty of finger pointing and accusations. Conrad thinks Gina has the bonsai tree. She still thinks it's hidden in her bedroom. Both Gina and Conrad suspect Maxine to have a strong motive to kill Harry. And Conrad just seems to be way too involved in all the shenanigans. You know, all three of them were at the auction. It's just a question of who had the strongest motive to lure Harry to the edge of the woods and stab him."

Fear filled his eyes, an elusive emotion Hitch rarely showed. "Is that what this is about, Sunny? I hope you know what you're doing because, as far as Officer Walker is concerned, I had opportunity and motive. This plan could completely backfire."

I hadn't considered that. And, since Hitch took the bonsai tree out of Gina's bedroom, he was the only one who knew where it was now. *She* didn't even know it was gone. What can of worms had I opened with this ill-thought-out plan?

"Sunny?" Tilly joined us in the kitchen. "Charlotte's ready to see those kittens you promised to show her. Are you ready?"

"You take her and Gina, Tilly. I'll drive over to the greenhouse with Hitch and Conrad. Okay?"

"Sure. That works. Hey, you know I'm not one to pry, but what's going on? You two look like you just swallowed a fishing hook instead of those delicious cookies. And, by the way, Sunny, you need to make more of them. Just sayin'." She winked and waited with her hands on her hips. "Well?"

"Well, nothing, Tilly." I said. I didn't see any point in rehashing everything Hitch and I had just talked about. "How were Gina and Conrad acting when they first showed up here? I can't figure out if they hate each other or are in cahoots against the rest of us."

Tilly moved closer and put her finger to her lips, glancing back toward the living room.

"Shhh." She whispered, "I'm glad you asked because there's something fishier than the chowder at the Little Dog Diner going on with those two. They've completely ignored Charlotte, letting me take care of all her needs. And this is the kicker. They're both on the phone tap, tap, tapping away constantly. I think they're sending messages to each other so they can communicate and keep us in the dark."

"Interesting," I said. "Gina tried to convince me that Maxine and Conrad are working together. I'd sure love to get a look at her phone."

A grin spread across Tilly's face. "Leave that task to me. If there's an opportunity, I'll snag her phone so fast she won't know what happened."

"We'd better get going, Sunny." Hitch added. "Maxine won't wait there forever. I told her a half hour, and it's well past that, now."

Tilly's ears perked up. "Maxine? What's that about?"

Hitch rolled his eyes. I wished he wouldn't do that. At least not when I was looking, but maybe that was his plan so I'd know exactly what he thought about my plan. He didn't like it.

"Sunny wants all the people that had any contact with Harry at our new property at the same time — Gina, Conrad, and Maxine. And, by default, I'm in that group too, which doesn't make me comfortable."

Tilly held onto Hitch's arm. "I almost forgot to ask. Where is the bonsai tree?"

"Safely hidden," Hitch answered and walked past Tilly.

"Uh-oh," Tilly said. "Trouble in paradise."

"Not exactly trouble. Yet. And, definitely not paradise. I think Hitch is overreacting," I said, but deep down? I was worried, too.

32

*H*itch's prediction was right.

Trouble waited in the parking lot when we arrived to meet Maxine.

In the form of Officer Mick Walker.

But it wasn't all bad news because Tilly had arrived before us and in true Tilly form, she was putting on some kind of show.

Conrad studied her from the front seat. "She's quite entertaining, isn't she?"

"The thing about Tilly is that you never know what she'll do or say next. But nine times out of ten there's a purpose to her madness," Hitch said as we watched the activity through the windshield of my car. He opened his door, "Showtime."

Conrad turned around to look at me in the back seat. "What's he mean by that?"

"I'm not sure, but maybe we'll find out what Tilly's up to. Let's go and find out. Oh," I put my hand on his shoulder, stopping him from leaving. "You knew the details about Harry's insurance policy on the bonsai tree, right?"

He nodded.

"Was there anybody named as a beneficiary if he died?"

"As far as I know, the plant was insured for theft as long as Harry had all the security measures in place. Once he moved his collection to Maxine's house, I assume that policy would be void. It's possible that Maxine talked Harry into getting a new policy, but they never told me about it."

Interesting. I wished I could see the expression on his face. "Are you upset about that? I mean, you *are* Harry's son, and he kept you in the insurance scam loop but not for these latest decisions? That sure would make me spit a few nails."

I liked that image, especially imagining Conrad the contractor shooting nails at Maxine.

He squirmed in his seat. His jaw muscles clenched and unclenched. "Harry was a selfish, greedy, manipulator. But if you're thinking you can pin his murder on me, you're dead wrong."

He opened the door, got out, and slammed it behind him.

"Well, that went well, didn't it, Jasper?" I'd

managed to upset Conrad in a big way. "Come on, big girl, let's see what Tilly's got up her sleeve." I was beginning to feel a little better about gathering these people together. If nothing else, she'd flush *something* out from under a rock.

It didn't take long to get close enough to the group to hear Tilly's bluster. "And you know what happened then, Mick?"

Everyone stared at her. Me included.

Officer Walker opened his mouth, probably to tell Tilly to be quiet so *he* could ask the questions, but she only took a quick breath before she continued. "I saw Maxine push Harry and yell at him."

Mick looked at Maxine. "Is that true?"

"I didn't *push* him, Mick. I only jabbed him with my finger. He was supposed to bid on that property, but he let *Sunny* buy it." The dirty look Maxine shot in my direction made me wonder if my name tasted like poison to her.

"We had big plans. Of course, I was upset." At least the spotlight was off of Hitch.

"Yeah," Tilly continued. "Mick, ask her about that insurance policy she took out on the very valuable bonsai tree." She managed to send me a quick smirk when Mick's attention turned to Maxine.

Maxine's mouth fell down to her chest. "How do you know about that?" She looked at Mick, his face as red as the sad pot of blooming poppies sitting in the weeds. "You told them?"

Tilly wiped her hands together as if she was gladly getting rid of dirt. "That's why I asked Hitch to call you to meet us here, Maxine. I knew you wouldn't come if *I* asked. What *is* the whole story on that insurance policy?"

I caught Hitch's attention, hoping he heard Tilly's comment taking responsibility for the phone call. He wiped his brow like he knew he'd dodged a bullet.

"Maxine?" Mick asked, taking her arm and turning her so she was forced to face him. "Did you tell me everything?"

"Yes." She looked away. In a lower, childlike voice she said, "Sort of. Harry extended the insurance policy, at my request. But that was only because I didn't want all that responsibility. I have a security system, and, well, I did fudge a little about saying I had a security guard, but I never thought the tree would get stolen to begin with. It was a just in case thing I told Harry. I'm trying desperately to get it back, Mick."

"Sure, she is." Tilly snickered. "She probably made Harry put the policy in her name."

I couldn't figure out how Tilly knew all this. Unless, she was just winging it like she usually did and happened to be right.

"Maxine?" Mick asked again, but this time there was an undertone of anger simmering in his tone. Apparently, insurance fraud was a line he wasn't willing to cross.

Maxine stomped her foot. I'd seen her do that before when she'd run out of excuses. She was such a drama queen.

"Yes. It's in my name but it will turn up. That's why I rushed over here when Hitch called, and why I wanted you here, too. To keep him honest."

She shot Hitch a glare. "He said he had information about my bonsai tree. I thought he knew where it was. I didn't know that *Tilly* was behind the call."

Keep Hitch honest? That sounded like projecting to me, and I barely managed to stop myself from strangling her.

"It's *your* bonsai tree now?" Conrad said, catching Maxine's slip of the tongue. "Did Harry give it to you or just name you on the insurance policy?"

"Oh, you know what I meant. Harry didn't *give* it to me. I agreed to keep his plants in my conservatory until he bought the old Nine Pine Nursery. That was the deal, and he didn't do his part."

"So, you killed him!" Tilly yelled. "You've always had to get your way, Maxine. Harry just didn't live up to your demands."

Maxine stared at Tilly, shaking her head and backing away from everyone. "I don't intend to stand here listening to any more of your ridiculous speculation. I didn't kill Harry, and I hope that bonsai tree never sees the inside of my conservatory again. It's been nothing but trouble."

She stomped to her flashy Lexus and sent dirt flying when she hit the gas.

I stared as my brain tried to catch up with what just happened.

Tilly, on her tippy toes, pointed her finger in Mick's face and yelled, "You just let the murderer drive off. Go follow her!"

He hesitated, then to my utter shock, he got in his car and left.

"What just happened?" Conrad asked, as confused as I was.

Tilly waved off the whole thing like it was merely a pesky swarm of bees she'd managed to save us from.

"Those kittens, Sunny?" she asked, with a nod toward my building.

How could I have forgotten? I looked at the door just as Jasper, apparently impatient with our dawdling, nosed her way through the door and disappeared inside. The kittens were front and center for her.

"Charlotte?" Tilly gently held Charlotte's arm and led her toward the door.

"This is so exciting," she said, looking at Tilly like she was the best thing that had ever happened to her.

"Riding in that green bug, and now, kittens? I can't imagine my life being any better than this."

Conrad and Gina stood off to one side, eyeing Charlotte and then the two vehicles—mine and Tilly's. I used my fob to lock my car and hoped Tilly had done the same instead of her usual habit of leaving the key in the ignition.

"Not thinking of taking a little trip, are you?" I asked them.

Conrad guided Gina toward the door. He smiled as he walked by me.

"Of course not."

"Before we go inside," I said, "I'm wondering if this belongs to either one of you." I pulled the watch with the broken strap out of my pocket and dangled it in front of their eyes.

Gina looked away. Conrad's eyes widened slightly. "Where'd you get that?" he asked.

"Did you lose it?" I asked.

"No." He glanced at Gina, studying her face but didn't say anything. I couldn't figure out those two.

I shoved it back in my pocket. "Ready to go inside?"

"Whatever," Gina said.

Right. Whatever was her response about this whole confusing mess.

---

33

*C*onrad walked beside Hitch. "I'd still like to help with the remodeling," Conrad said. "It won't take long to transform the greenhouse into Sunny's Kitty Castle dream. The sooner it happens, the quicker you'll find homes for those kittens while they're small and irresistible."

Hitch shoved his hands into his pockets and stared at the ground. I wished I could read his mind. I wanted to hear Conrad's ideas, but Hitch had to be on board, too. Sure, we could work hard and do all the clean-up, but with a real contractor handling any building permits and regulations, we'd do it right the first time.

Gina moved at a snail's pace. I didn't dare let her out of my sight, so I slowed down, too, as we barely inched our way to the door.

"So?" Gina interrupted my thoughts. "Will you take me home now? Charlotte's all gaga over Tilly and couldn't care less if I'm here or not. I don't need this right now."

"Don't need what, Gina?" I faced her. "To do the right thing and reconnect with your grandmother when she needs help? What is it with you? You pulled her out of the nursing home where she was content, and now you're ready to dump her on the side of the road like an unwanted kitten?"

"No. It's not that." She sighed and her body shrank. "I don't think I can do it. I didn't know how hard it would be. I have to work, and I can't be with her all day."

I had to admit that she had a point but her whining grated. I forced that aside and said, "I'm sure Tilly will help. Maybe Charlotte could stay with her during the day and with you at night?"

She brightened at that suggestion. "You think Tilly would do that? I mean, I can't pay her, at least not unless I sell the bonsai tree, and Hitch would have to help me with that. I guess I could grovel and go back to Maxine. She might take me back, or I could find a different cleaning job if she refuses."

I put my arm around her shoulder. "You don't have to do it alone, Gina. Make a schedule and ask for help."

She nodded. "Okay."

"Come on then. I want to see how the kittens are doing. They have a special magic that will make you feel better no matter what's happening." I pulled her along through the building into the greenhouse.

Tilly had found an ancient but sturdy chair for Charlotte. She had a heck of a time corralling several kittens on her lap. They climbed up her arms and over the chair, but she laughed and managed to keep them from falling off.

Conrad held Mama Cat, who looked perfectly content to get a break along with the cuddles. With his obvious love of cats, I couldn't think of anyone better to help us design the Kitty Castle.

Hitch whispered in my ear. "I know what you're thinking, Sunshine," he said, a twinkle in his eye. "Conrad is trying his hardest to win me over. He knows you've got a soft spot for him. But," he pulled me away from the others and lowered his voice even more, "he thinks Gina has the bonsai tree hidden somewhere. What if he's trying to cozy up to us to cut him some slack to find the tree?"

"He's in for a surprise then, isn't he? Especially since Gina doesn't know where the tree is anymore." I laughed at that deception Hitch had pulled off. "I think I convinced Gina to make a plan for caring for Charlotte. I said we'd pitch in, and that calmed her down. She said she needs your help to sell the bonsai tree, so she has money for Charlotte's care. How hard will that be?"

Hitch shrugged. "I have some names, but we don't even know who it belongs to."

"And look at this one, Charlotte." Tilly handed over the smallest of the kittens, the mostly gray one with intense blue eyes. The first one Jasper had found.

Charlotte's face glowed with happiness. Having one of the kittens at Gina's house would keep her content, I decided. Maybe that little one would do the trick.

And then, for some reason, she lurched to one side.

Like a slow-motion film, Charlotte's chair tipped precariously. I jumped around Hitch to catch it, but Jasper chose that moment to walk between Charlotte and me. Instead of saving her from a fall, I found myself sprawled in the dirt next to her with kittens crawling over me.

Charlotte groaned.

"Hitch!" Tilly yelled. "Help me over here."

First, he pulled me to my feet, then bent down to help Charlotte. He carefully put one arm under her legs, and the other under her arms while Tilly righted the chair. Hitch lowered Charlotte safely back on the seat.

"I'm fine. Don't worry," she insisted but I saw scrapes on her hand that needed to be cleaned.

I got the water bowl I'd brought for the kittens, filled it with clean water, and handed it to Tilly. She dipped the hem of her skirt in the bowl and dabbed at Charlotte's hand.

"Hey." I looked around. "Where'd Gina and Conrad go?"

"Check outside," Hitch said. "I'll stay here to help Tilly."

I ran outside with Jasper, only to discover Tilly's lime green VW gone.

They'd taken off.

"Come on, Jasper." As I ran toward my car, I pointed the fob and unlocked the door, let Jasper in the back, and got behind the wheel. If Tilly left her key in the car, Gina, no doubt, filed that away for her getaway plan. I kicked myself for not checking. I assumed Gina made a beeline home when she saw we were distracted with Charlotte.

Unless Conrad had a different plan.

I drove to Gina's house to check there first.

As I turned onto her street, Maxine's Lexus was parked in Gina's driveway next to Gina's old sedan.

Strange. What was Maxine doing here? And where was Tilly's Volkswagen?

I screeched to a stop. I needed to focus on figuring this out before Gina completely disappeared with Tilly's car. I refused to let her abandon her responsibility to her grandmother during this critical transition time. On top of that, I needed to find out what Maxine knew.

Outside the car, a mower buzzed somewhere in the neighborhood, chickadees tweeted in the trees, and the wind ruffled the leaves, but those every day sounds only registered in the far back of my brain. With Jasper at my side, we ran to the front door. I knocked and called, "Gina? Maxine? Are you there?

The deep silence from within was interrupted by Jasper's bark. She ran along the front of the house and I followed her as she disappeared into the backyard.

My stomach lurched. There was Tilly's Volkswagen, scratched and dented, parked under the shade of a big maple tree. It was missing the side mirror and a branch stuck out from the front grill. Oh, Tilly. I could just hear her furious rant when she saw the damage to her precious bug.

Jasper scratched at the backdoor. I peeked through the window into Gina's kitchen. My heart pounded at the sight of Maxine crumpled on the floor, blood oozing from her head. Someone else *had* to be here.

I couldn't even begin to guess what happened, but it wasn't good. With shaky fingers, I punched in

9-1-1, then sent a message to Hitch: *come to Gina's house.*

I leaned against the wall next to the door wondering what to do when I heard a crash inside.

I turned the knob and cracked the door. Could I sneak in quietly? Jasper had other ideas. She pushed through and raced inside.

I followed, scared, but knowing help was on its way.

34

*J*asper didn't wait for me to catch up to her. She rushed through Gina's kitchen, weaving around knocked over chairs, on a mission of her own.

As I followed, anxious to stay close to her, Maxine groaned. I kneeled down next to her as Jasper disappeared into another room. Maxine's eyes fluttered. "Maxine? It's me, Sunny. What happened?"

Her eyes opened, and she gave me a terrified look when they focused on me. She mumbled, "Help."

"Help is coming," I said, holding her cold hand. I didn't dare try to move her. "What happened?"

"Tree," she managed to say before her eyes closed.

Tree? Did Maxine come here looking for the bonsai tree?

I heard a door slam upstairs, and Jasper barked ferociously.

I hesitated, torn between staying with Maxine and finding what Jasper was up to. Maybe Gina was upstairs in some kind of trouble. Maybe Conrad had her locked in a room. But I couldn't abandon Maxine yet.

I searched the kitchen for something to cover her shivering body with, and yanked the tablecloth off a small table, sending a plate sailing off and shattering when it hit the floor. Maxine flinched.

As I leaned over her, tucking the cloth around her as best I could. The watch in my pocket popped out and landed in her open palm.

Lifting the object to see what it was, Maxine mumbled, "Harry," before her hand fell to her chest.

I saw an identical, but smaller watch, on her wrist and slipped it off. Both had identical hearts engraved on the back. What did it mean?

And then, everything fell into place.

A chill seeped into my bones.

I slipped Maxine's watch back on her wrist and folded her fingers over the other one. Harry's watch.

"I'll be back," I whispered, hoping she'd be fine until then.

I followed Jasper's woofing up the stairs, my

footsteps muffled by her barks. "Gina?" I yelled at the closed door. "Are you all right?"

The door opened a crack, an arm came out and pulled me inside before I knew what happened. The door slammed closed. Jasper, still on the wrong side of the door escalated her jumping and scratching at the door, frantic to follow me.

Gina, alone in her bedroom, pushed me onto a chair. "Where is it?" she demanded as she looked around the room, wild-eyed and frantic but keeping her steely grip on my arm.

"What are you talking about?" I had to distract her until the police arrived.

"The bonsai tree, you do-gooder. When I left, it was here in my room. Where is it? Tell me or you'll get the same treatment Maxine got when I found her sneaking into my house. She didn't find it either."

"It's too late, Gina. The police are on the way." I kept my voice calm even though my insides were twisted in knots.

She went silent and tilted her head toward the open window. We couldn't hear anything over Jasper's barking. "You're lying. Why would you call the police?"

"Because you killed Harry to get his bonsai tree," I said.

"You're bluffing. Conrad stole the bonsai from

Maxine and put it in my car. I was only protecting it."

"That was so convenient for you, wasn't it? He gave you exactly what you coveted. And, you played the misunderstood granddaughter to get Tilly and me to help you." I stared at her, not showing any fear.

"You made a big mistake, Gina. You shouldn't have stolen Harry's watch when you stabbed him. But I shouldn't be surprised. Your greediness knows no bounds, does it? You'll steal from anyone. Including your own grandmother."

Gina, agitated, paced between the door and my chair. Her knuckles white from the death grip she had on her phone. "Charlotte did *nothing* for me. She *owes* me that bonsai tree."

And there it was, the truth coming out like it always does.

"No one *owes* you a thing, Gina. Is that what you argued with Harry about? You demanded the bonsai tree after you heard him talking to Maxine about how valuable it is. You saw your opportunity to get rich quick."

Her face twisted into a sneer. "When he saw me at the auction, he finally put two and two together. Yeah, he saw me at Maxine's house. I lied to you about that."

"All you're good at is lying, Gina."

She continued, her eyes glassy. "Harry promised to tell Maxine to fire me so I couldn't even *look* at his precious tree. Then, he laughed right in my face." She stopped her manic pacing and picked up a heavy lamp, throwing the shade across the room. "I had no choice but to stab him after I lured him behind some trees. I'd had enough of him trying to control my life. He didn't even die right away, the fool. He tried to get help." She lifted the lamp. "*You* won't be so lucky."

As she swung it at my head, I jumped to the side. The force sent Gina and the lamp crashing to the floor. Her phone skidded away from her. She scurried to her feet, ran to the window, and threw her leg over the sill. I had no intention of stopping her, knowing she wouldn't get far.

After she disappeared from my sight, I went to the window and watched her shimmy down a tree right into the waiting arms of Officer Mick Walker. I had to admit this was probably the first time in my life that I was thrilled to see him. But he'd never hear *that* from my lips.

I scooped up Gina's phone and opened the door. Jasper, making another lunge at the same time, flew through the opening and bowled me over. She covered me with licks, which I didn't try to avoid this time. I was just happy to be unharmed.

When I could finally see around Jasper's enormous body, there was Hitch, resting against the doorframe grinning at me. His smile made the edges of his eyes crinkle so delightfully, I forgot all about Gina.

"What happened?" he asked casually, as if I hadn't just escaped a psychopath.

"Gina came back for the bonsai tree. You were right, Hitch. We needed it to flush out the killer."

I held out my hand and he pulled me to my feet. Jasper, still glued to my side, made for an awkward trip down the stairs.

I glanced at Gina's phone. "Now, I see what she was up to," I said to Hitch, showing him a string of reservations she'd made at a motels across the country. "It looks like she planned to disappear with the bonsai tree… except she couldn't find it." I looked at him. "Where is it?"

Hitch led me through the kitchen, now empty, and the chairs tucked under the table. "Come on. I'll show you."

We walked out the back door, passed Tilly's car, to the far corner of Gina's yard. He slid a round table top off an empty oak barrel and there, nestled inside, was Harry's bonsai tree. Safe and sound.

"Amazing. What a perfect hiding spot."

"Yeah, I didn't have much time. I guess it's my lucky day."

I had to agree.

"What happened to my car?" Tilly yelled, making Hitch and I turn around.

"Oh boy," I said. "This won't end well."

Tilly walked around rubbing each scratch, ding, and dent before puckering her lips and saying, "I always wanted a convertible. This is the sign I've been waiting for to trade this baby in and live my dream."

"A sign? Somehow, she manages to turn any disaster completely around," I whispered to Hitch.

He shrugged. "You never know what's going on in that mind of hers." He knocked me with his elbow. "Come on, we've got a plant to deliver."

He carefully picked up the bonsai tree and I followed him out front. "Conrad gave me a ride to get my truck."

"Conrad?" I'd forgotten all about him. "He disappeared at the same time Gina left. I thought they were together."

"Nope. She left him in the dust. Once he saw that watch, and recognized it as Harry's, he suspected what Gina was up to and called Maxine."

"And she came here looking for the bonsai tree, getting bashed over the head trying to rescue it," I filled in. "How is she?"

"She'll be fine. I promised to bring the tree to her conservatory for safe-keeping. And you won't believe what she offered."

"What?"

"She said that Charlotte can live with her so she can enjoy her orchids and the bonsai tree for the rest of her life."

"Maxine's going to take care of Charlotte?" I could barely get the words out. I was completely and utterly flabbergasted.

Hitch chuckled and held his hands up to stop me from having a heart attack. "Not exactly. She'll provide a nice apartment for Charlotte and a live-in companion."

Officer Walker approached us. "You know you put yourself in danger, Sunny."

"It was all Jasper's fault. She pushed Gina's kitchen door open and I'd planned to stay with Maxine until she recognized the watch."

"What watch?"

"Harry's watch. Jasper found it, Maxine recognized it, and I figured out what Gina had done."

Mick shook his head. He ruffled Jasper's ears. "So, Jasper saved the day?"

"Sort of. She led me to the killer, but she got herself locked out of the room when Gina pulled me inside. Fortunately for me, Gina didn't have much of a plan in place when everything started to fall apart."

"Except for this." Hitch handed Mick the phone. "She made motel reservations, in Charlotte's name and probably used her credit card," he pointed out, "from here to New Mexico. I don't think her car would have made it. She didn't have the bonsai tree, but I guess she saw the writing on the wall and knew it was time to disappear."

"Nice catch, by the way," I said to Mick. "She climbed right down into your arms, didn't she?"

"That was the easiest arrest I've ever made."

"You're welcome," I said.

He patted my shoulder. "Yeah, thanks. Now, go deliver that gnarled old tree before it causes any more trouble. I'll catch up with you tomorrow for the rest of your details." He walked away mumbling to himself, probably wishing he'd been the one to rescue me instead of me defending myself quite handily.

"Yup, that tree has a permanent home now. And, you know what else, Sunshine?" Hitch looked at me with a gleam in his eyes that made me a little worried about what might come out next.

"Do I want to know?"

He laughed again. "We're partners. Of course you want to know. Why are you so suspicious?"

I shrugged. "Your track record?"

"Well, I know I have a lot of work to do to make you forgive me for running off to New York, but I think you'll like what I'm about to propose."

I held my breath, preparing myself for disappointment.

"I asked Conrad to give us a quote on turning the greenhouse into your Kitty Castle."

I felt my mouth spread into a gigantic grin.

"Good, right? He's already working on the plans and wants to get started as soon as possible. And," Hitch said, "He wants to adopt Mama Cat when the kittens are all on their own. What do you think?"

"I'm glad that Conrad is one of the good guys."

"What about me?" His face fell into a pout.

"You still have work to do, Hitch... lots of work."

He took my hand and squeezed, sending my heart fluttering against my ribs. That was a good start.

But I wasn't planning to tell him that anytime soon.

MORE BLUEBERRY BAY

Welcome to Blueberry Bay, a scenic region of Maine peppered with quaint small towns and home to a shocking number of mysteries. If you loved this book, then make sure to check out its sister series from other talented Cozy Mystery authors...

Pet Whisperer P.I.
By Molly Fitz

Glendale is home to Blueberry Bay's first ever talking cat detective. Along with his ragtag gang of human and animal helpers, Octo-Cat is determined to save the day... so long as it doesn't interfere with his schedule. Start with book one, *Kitty Confidential*,

which is now available to buy or borrow! Visit Visit
www.QuirkyCozy.com/PetWhisperer for more.

Little Dog Diner
By Emmie Lyn

Misty Harbor boasts the best lobster rolls in all of
Blueberry Bay. There's another thing that's always
on the menu, too. Murder! Dani and her little
terrier, Pip, have a knack for being in the wrong
place at the wrong time... which often lands them
smack in the middle of a fresh, new murder mystery
and in the crosshairs of one cunning criminal after
the next. Start with book one, *Mixing Up Murder*,
which is now available to buy or borrow! Visit
www.QuirkyCozy.com/LittleDog for more.

Shelf Indulgence
By S.E. Babin

Dewdrop Springs is home to Tattered Pages, a
popular bookshop specializing in rare editions, a
grumpy Persian cat named Poppy, and some of the
most suspicious characters you'll ever meet. And

poor Dakota Adair has just inherited it all. She'll need to make peace with her new cat and use all her book smarts to catch a killer or she might be the next to wind up dead in the stacks. Start with book one, *Hardback Homicide*, which is now available to buy or borrow! Visit www.QuirkyCozy.com/Shelf-Indulgence for more.

Haunted Housekeeping
By R.A. Muth

Cooper's Cove is home to Blueberry Bay's premier estate cleaning service. Tori and Hazel, the ill-fated proprietors of Bubbles and Troubles, are prepared to uncover a few skeletons. But when a real one turns up, they'll have to solve the mystery quickly if they're going to save their reputations—and their lives. Book one, *The Squeaky Clean Skeleton*, will be coming soon. Keep an eye on www.QuirkyCozy.-com/HauntedHousekeeping for more.

The Cursed Cat of Caraway
By F.M. Storm

Quiet, secluded, and most importantly, far away from his annoying magical family, Guy couldn't wait to start a new life on Caraway Island. Unfortunately, he hadn't counted on his four-year-old daughter coming into her own witchy powers early... or on her accidentally murdering one of the PTO moms. Oops! Book one, *The Kindergarten Coven*, will be coming soon. Keep an eye on www.QuirkyCozy.com/CursedCat for more.

MORE EMMIE!

I hope you enjoyed this book.

Click here to sign up for my newsletter and never miss a new release.

About Emmie Lyn

Emmie Lyn shares her world with her husband, a rescue terrier named Underdog, and a black cat named Ziggy. When she's not busy thinking of ways to kill off a character, she loves enjoying tea and chocolate in her flower garden, hiking, or spending time near the ocean.

Emmielynbooks.com

More from Emmie

COZY MYSTERIES

Little Dog Diner Cozy Mystery Series

Mixing Up Murder

Serving Up Suspects

Dishing Up Deceit

Cooking Up Chaos

Crumbling Up Crooks

Dicing Up Disaster

Mint Chocolate Chip Mysteries

Claws of Justice

Coming in 2020

Ginger Danger

Tabby Trouble

Tuxedo Bravado

Furrgone Conclusion

Romantic Suspense

Gold Coast Retriever Series

Helping Hanna

Shielding Shelly